LUCKY

LUCKY

MARIS, MANTLE,
AND
MY BEST SUMMER EVER

WES TOOKE

SIMON & SCHUSTER BOOKS FOR YOUNG READERS
NEW YORK   LONDON   TORONTO   SYDNEY

SIMON & SCHUSTER BOOKS FOR YOUNG READERS
An imprint of Simon & Schuster Children's Publishing Division
1230 Avenue of the Americas, New York, New York 10020

SIMON & SCHUSTER BOOKS FOR YOUNG READERS is a trademark of Simon & Schuster, Inc.
For information about special discounts for bulk purchases, please contact Simon & Schuster Special Sales at 1-866-506-1949 or business@simonandschuster.com.
The Simon & Schuster Speakers Bureau can bring authors to your live event. For more information or to book an event, contact the Simon & Schuster Speakers Bureau at 1-866-248-3049 or visit our website at www.simonspeakers.com.
Book design by Krista Vossen
The text for this book is set in Melior.
Manufactured in the United States of America
0110 FFG
2 4 6 8 10 9 7 5 3 1
Library of Congress Cataloging-in-Publication Data
Tooke, Wes.
Lucky: Maris, Mantle, and My Best Summer Ever / Wes Tooke.—1st ed.
p. cm.
Summary: Louis, who loves baseball despite being the worst stickball player in White Plains, New York, sees his opportunity to be bat boy for the 1961 Yankees team as the perfect way to escape the problems of his father's remarriage and moving to the suburbs.
ISBN 978-1-4169-8663-8
[1. Baseball—Fiction. 2. Bat boys—Fiction. 3. Maris, Roger, 1934–1985—Fiction. 4. Mantle, Mickey, 1931–1995—Fiction. 5. New York Yankees (Baseball team)—Fiction. 6. Stepfamilies—Fiction. 7. Moving, Household—Fiction. 8. New York (State)—History—20th century—Fiction.] I. Title.
PZ7.T638Mae 2010
[Fic]—dc22
2009007150
ISBN 978-1-4391-5825-8 (eBook)

*In memory of Elvira Growdon, a generous reader
and an unwavering friend to children*

ACKNOWLEDGMENTS

This project began with an idea by Courtney Bongiolatti, who also served as the book's editor and improved the project in countless ways. I am greatly indebted to Simon Lipskar and Dan Lazar at Writers House for bringing the idea to me and to Dan for his guidance during its development. Thanks also to Katie Flynn, Heather McDonald, and Katherine Lieban for their careful reads and suggestions.

Finally, this book only exists because of the unwavering support of my family. Especially my wife. As always, the mistakes are mine, anything that remains is yours. . . .

LUCKY

Warm-up

In Louis's opinion nothing in the world contained more information in a smaller space than a baseball card. You could fit a whole season into a single line of numbers, and each of those numbers—just a few squiggles on a piece of paper—could ignite an entire scene in your imagination. Louis's brand-new 1961 Mickey Mantle card said that Mickey had hit 40 home runs in 1960, which meant that 40 times the bat had made a sharp *crack*, the pitcher had spun around, hands on his hips, an outfielder had stared glumly at the bleachers, the crowd had risen to gasp or cheer, a pack of teammates had leaped up from the bench—

"Louis!" a voice called.

It was his stepmother. She was probably at the top of the stairs, and Louis instinctively slid farther behind the shelter of his bed. He was squatted next to the window in the room that he shared with his stepbrother, the two shoe boxes that contained his card collection open on the floor in front of him. In Louis's right hand he held a small stack of current Yankees sorted by career home runs. Louis had to add in his head the homers the players had hit so far this season to the totals on the cards, which meant that Mickey Mantle had 345 instead of 320, Roger Maris had 136 instead of 109, Yogi Berra had—

"Louis!"

His stepmother was standing over him, a broom clutched in one hand, and for a moment Louis thought that she was going to sweep him out of the house. He began to gather the Yankees on the floor into a neat pile, his hands fumbling with the cards.

"I've been calling you from downstairs," she said. "Didn't you hear me?"

"No, ma'am."

Her blue eyes narrowed. "The kids have been playing stickball for over an hour."

The sound of the game had indeed been drifting through the open window in Louis's bedroom—shouts and laughter and the occasional solid *thwack* as the mop handle connected with the tennis ball—but Louis had done his best to ignore them. The previous afternoon he had made four errors in right field, each more embarrassing than the last.

"I forgot," he said.

His stepmother shook her head, the blond bobs of her hair moving in perfect unison. Louis's father liked to joke that she could walk through a hurricane and emerge with her hair perfectly combed and her blue-and-white checkered dress unruffled.

"I swear, Louis," she said. "You'd lose your head if it wasn't attached to your body."

"Yes, ma'am."

"Go outside with the other kids. There's more to life than baseball cards."

"I don't want to play."

"I wasn't asking, Louis. I was telling. Go play with your brother."

"Stepbrother," Louis said a little louder than he intended.

She gave him her fiercest look, the look that meant business, and Louis scooted downstairs. His stepmother was tricky. Sometimes, when she was staring at his dad across the kitchen table, she looked like a movie star. Sweet and kind and pretty. But when she got mad and her thin eyebrows gathered in the center of her forehead, she was meaner than any of the teachers at his old school—even Mrs. Lambert, who whacked at least one student with a ruler every day.

The neighborhood kids played stickball in the vacant lot behind Louis's house. An old mansion had burned in a fire, leaving only a large brick column that had once been the main chimney. Bryce, Louis's stepbrother, had designed the local rules. The game was exactly like baseball, except instead of a catcher and umpire there was just a chalk rectangle drawn on the chimney. If you didn't swing and the ball hit inside the rectangle, it was a strike.

As Louis approached the game, eight kids were standing in a line next to the chimney waiting to hit, and another nine were scattered around the field. The pitcher was tossing the tennis ball in his hand, waiting for the next batter to pick up the broomstick. Bryce was standing near the end of the line, his arms folded across his new Mickey Mantle jersey and his Yankee cap perched at a jaunty angle atop his tangle of curly blond hair. His blue eyes narrowed just like his mother's when he noticed Louis.

"I thought you didn't want to play," he said.

"I don't. Your mom said I have to."

Bryce pointed at the thick grass of the outfield. "Go out there."

Louis slid his glove onto his hand and took a few steps onto the field. The pitcher, a gangly kid in jeans and a white T-shirt, stepped forward, shaking his head.

"You take him," he said. "We already have enough players."

The pitcher was staring past Louis to Bryce, but Bryce was silent. This was the moment that Louis hated the most—everyone watching him and praying that he wouldn't end up on their team.

"Fine," Bryce finally said. "But he hits last."

Louis gratefully stepped to the end of the line. Hitting last was fine. In fact, he wouldn't mind if the game ended before he had to hit at all. Bryce nevertheless gave him a dirty look, which Louis tried to ignore. Bryce was mad because Louis's father—Bryce's stepfather—was taking Louis to a game at Yankee Stadium that afternoon. It wasn't fair for Bryce to be mad because he had gotten to go to a game the previous weekend, but Bryce could get mad for any reason, fair or not. And when he got mad, he almost always got his way.

The stickball games lasted only seven innings, and they were already in the bottom of the sixth when Louis arrived. Three kids on Louis's team made quick outs, and when they took the field Bryce told Louis to return to right—the scene of his fielding crimes the previous day. Mercifully, no batter hit a ball in his direction, and Louis spent the top of the inning kicking weeds and trying to figure out if he would have to hit. He was the sixth batter in line and they were down two runs, which meant that unless three kids got on base he was safe.

From Louis's perspective the bottom of the seventh began perfectly. The first batter popped up to the shortstop, and the second batter grounded out to first. But the third batter hit a dribbler down the third-base line, so soft it was almost a bunt, and easily beat the throw. The fourth batter hit a solid single to center, and the fifth batter was Bryce—who always got a hit. This time he drove the ball past the first baseman, and suddenly Louis was standing at the plate, the tying run on third, and Bryce—the winning run—on second.

"Why did he have to come?" someone behind him asked. "Now we're going to lose."

"He couldn't hit water if he fell out of a boat," someone else said.

Louis tried to ignore the comments as he settled into his crouch. Bryce had wrapped tape around one end of the broom to make a handle, and the grip was warm and sticky in his hands. The science of hitting was simple. Since the bat weighs more than the ball, all you need to do is make clean contact and most of the energy from the collision will transfer to the ball and—

"Strike one!" the shortstop shouted.

Louis blinked. The tennis ball was bouncing back toward the pitcher's mound.

"Open your eyes!" Bryce yelled.

Bryce was standing on the cardboard box that was second base as if he were claiming the base for Spain. Nobody would ever mistake Louis and Bryce for real brothers. Louis had olive skin, thick black hair, and eyes so brown that it was hard to tell his pupils from his irises. But the differences between the boys went beyond the way they looked or Bryce's extra year of age. When they were playing stickball, Bryce acted like a real ballplayer; he wore the right clothes and talked the right way and pounded his glove and spat in the dirt, and when he made a mistake and dropped a fly ball, nobody ever said anything because—

"Strike two!" the shortstop shouted.

The tennis ball was again bouncing back toward the mound. This time the pitcher was grinning, and Louis could hear a rumble of nasty comments from the line behind him.

"Come on, Louis," Bryce yelled from second. "Don't strike out."

That was a stupid thing to say, Louis thought. He had no control over whether or not he struck out. He was a bad player and that's what bad players did. They struck out or weakly bounced the ball back to the pitcher or—if they were very lucky—got a walk or were hit by the pitch. Occasionally they managed to dribble the ball to the perfect spot and get a cheap hit, but Louis's cheap hits only came early in the game or when nobody was on base. He wasn't lucky.

Louis suddenly realized that the pitcher was in his windup, and he gripped the bat a little tighter. This time he was going to swing. He was going to swing and he was going to change his luck, and nobody was going to be able to blame him. The ball was streaking toward the plate, a faint yellow blur, and Louis whipped the mop handle forward, his hands and hips moving together just like a real ballplayer—

"Game over!" the shortstop shouted.

Louis blinked. The other team was celebrating, and Bryce was trudging off the field, his cap in his hand.

"That was a foot outside," one of the kids said from the line.

"More like ten feet," another kid said. "He couldn't have hit that ball if he was swinging with a tree."

Louis picked up his glove, trying to ignore the comments, and slunk back toward his house. When he got there, Bryce was waiting on the porch.

"Sorry," Louis said.

Bryce glared at him for a long moment before turning and stepping inside. He spoke over his shoulder as he disappeared through the screen door. "You're the worst player in White Plains."

He said it calmly, like it was a fact. Louis wanted to reply with something clever, some comeback that would make him feel better about the strikeout, but there was nothing that he could say. Bryce was right. He was the worst player in White Plains. In fact, he was probably the worst player in New York—or maybe even the whole world.

CHAPTER ONE

Top of the First

L ouis sat next to his father in the second row of Yankee Stadium, roughly even with the third-base bag. His father was talking with one of his clients as Louis filled out a scorecard. This was the fifth game that Louis had attended this season. The first three had been during the Yankees' sluggish start, but the fourth had come during the furious stretch when the team shot into second place behind the Tigers. Louis believed that you could always tell how the team was doing just by the mood in the stadium. During a losing streak the crowd was quick to boo or heckle the players, but now, with the team surging, everyone was cheering even though the Yankees were trailing the Washington Senators by a run.

Louis loved everything about being at a baseball game. His favorite moment was when he first emerged from the tunnel into the stands. His eyes would leap to a thousand little details: the white chalk of the lines or the bunting on the upper deck or the perfect parabola where the smooth dirt of the infield surrendered to the emerald grass of the outfield. He would smell popcorn and the greasy steam of hot dogs, and the roar in his ears would swell from the reverberating chatter of the concourse to the hollow echo of the stands. And the best part was that the whole game, nine glorious innings, lay ahead of you.

But now, Louis glumly thought, only three outs remained. Three outs before the train back to White Plains and his stepmother and Bryce. Three outs before another few weeks of baseball being just a box score, a voice on the radio, or a lousy game of stickball. If Louis were more selfish, he might have prayed that the Yankees would tie the game in the bottom of the ninth so that he could watch a few more innings, but he was a true fan. He wanted two quick runs and a win.

As the Senators took the field, Louis's father tapped him on the knee. Even though it was Saturday, his father was wearing a white dress shirt and a black tie that matched the rims of his thick glasses. Everyone except Louis's stepmother always said that Louis and his father looked alike: brown eyes and hair, big noses, thick eyebrows, and feet as enormous and awkward as water skis.

"Tell Mr. Evans about the World Series game we saw last year," he said.

Louis kept his eyes on the field, but he spoke loudly because his father got mad when he mumbled to clients.

"Game three," he said. "Ten to zero. Whitey pitched. Bobby Richardson and Mickey hit home runs."

"It was a good game," Mr. Evans said. "And a better series."

"Mr. Evans is from Pittsburgh," Louis's father said.

Louis felt a pang in his stomach when he heard the word "Pittsburgh." The Pirates had beaten the Yankees in the seventh game of the World Series the previous season on a walk-off home run. The home run wasn't even by Roberto Clemente or Dick Groat, it was by stupid Bill Mazeroski, a second baseman. Louis's father must have sensed that he was upset because he put a gentle hand on Louis's shoulder.

"The Yankees should have won that series," he said. "Tell Mr. Evans what you keep telling me."

"The Yankees had all the numbers," Louis said. "They outscored the Pirates fifty-five to twenty-seven. It was just bad luck that all the runs came in the same games."

"I'm sure that's true," Mr. Evans said. "But let me give you a piece of advice, Louis. Sometimes life is about timing."

The Senators pitcher had finished warming up, and the Yankees second baseman, Tony Kubek, stepped into the batter's box. The first pitch was high and outside.

"Who's this pitcher?" Louis's father asked.

Louis wanted to ignore the question and focus on the game, but he knew what his father wanted. The reason his company bought the tickets was to entertain clients, which meant, as his father said, that sometimes he and Louis had to sing for their supper.

"Dave Sisler," Louis said. "Former pitcher for the Red Sox. Son of Gorgeous George Sisler, who holds the record for most hits in a single season."

"How does he know all that?" Mr. Evans asked Louis's father in a loud whisper.

"He studies baseball cards," Louis's father said.

The second pitch was on the inside corner, but Kubek whipped his hands around and drove a sharp single into right field. As he rounded first base, the crowd rose to its feet, a roar reverberating from the blue walls of the stadium. Roger Maris was striding to the plate, a bat slung over his shoulder. The sleeves of his white pinstriped uniform were shorter than the other players', which made his arms look long and lean in the gleaming late afternoon sun.

"We need Maris to get on base so Mantle can hit a home run," Louis's father said.

Mantle had already hit two home runs in the game, which meant that he was tied with Maris for the American League lead. All of the kids in Louis's neighborhood liked Mantle better and thought that he should have won the MVP the previous season instead of Maris, but Louis liked Maris. He was good at little things like getting a bunt down or throwing to the cutoff man. In Louis's most optimistic fantasies— fantasies in which he was actually good at baseball—he liked to imagine that he was a player like Maris: quiet, serious, dependable.

The first pitch was in the dirt. Maris kept one foot in the box as he adjusted his cap and then settled into his relaxed crouch. When he and Mantle were hitting well, they looked similar at the plate—calm and composed on the surface, but in their twitching bats you could see the energy of a coiled rattlesnake. Louis had occasionally stood in front of the mirror in his bedroom with a broomstick and tried to imitate their stance, but his shoulders always slouched too much, and the broomstick had all the energy of a wet noodle.

The second pitch was outside. Maris started his swing late and lunged toward the ball, his front shoulder dropping. Louis heard a hollow *crack* as the ball rose in the sky. People in his section started to stand, their heads tilted upward, and Louis dropped his lineup card and grabbed his glove. As he leaped onto his seat, Danny O'Connell, the Senators' veteran third baseman, leaned into the stands, his battered brown mitt stretching toward Louis's waist. Louis glanced up just in time to see a white streak. His hand, acting on instinct, twitched forward, and he heard a loud *pop* and felt a sting in his palm.

"Foul ball!" the umpire shouted.

Louis glanced down. Although his glove had folded with the force of the impact, a hint of a ball was nestled amid the worn leather of his webbing. Louis's mouth fell open. Had he really caught it? Was that possible?

"Hey!" O'Connell yelled. He was glaring at the umpire, his finger pointed at Louis. "That's fan interference!"

As O'Connell turned his anger toward the stands, Louis sank back into his seat. But the crowd rose to his defense. A man a few rows back yelled, "Hey, O'Connell, get lost," and as O'Connell opened his mouth his voice was drowned out by a cavalcade of boos. After a few seconds O'Connell shrugged, and as he walked over to the umpire, another man ruffled Louis's hair.

"That was an all-star play, kid," he said. "You stole it right out of that bum's glove."

Louis nodded, his eyes locked on the field. His cheeks

felt hot from the attention. O'Connell appeared to have lost the argument with the umpire because he gave the stands one last glare and then stalked back to third base. As Maris settled back into the batter's box, Louis glanced down at the ball. It was an even, dirty brown with just a single scuff mark on one of the fat parts of the leather.

"Great catch," his father said in his ear.

Louis felt himself flush. His father was always nice about his baseball cards and his grades, but that was the first time he'd ever said something like *great catch*. To be fair, Louis thought, that was probably the first *great catch* of his life. In fact, it was probably his first *good catch.* How had it happened? That ball had been a million times higher and fallen a million times faster than any of the balls in the stickball games, yet his hand had flashed forward just like a real ballplayer. Was it because he hadn't had time to think about it?

Louis turned his attention back to the field just in time to see Sisler start his windup. This time Maris timed his swing perfectly, and as the ball left the bat, he froze for an instant, his legs locked in a long stride and his hips pointed at center field. The man in the front row leaped to his feet, blocking Louis's view, but Louis knew from the roar of the crowd that the ball was headed for the right-field stands. A moment later people were pounding Louis on the back and leaping up and down, and Louis caught only a quick glimpse of Maris celebrating with a little crowd of teammates before he disappeared into the dugout.

"What a comeback!" Louis's father shouted over the pandemonium. "What a game!"

As the cheers slowly started to fade, Louis carefully marked the home run on his scorecard and tucked his pencil and the card into his pocket. A warm glow was filling his stomach and making the skin on his arms tingle. Maybe he hadn't done much; maybe he'd just gotten lucky and stuck his glove out at the right moment, but Louis still felt as if he'd contributed to the Yankees' comeback in some small way. He wondered if the kids in the neighborhood would believe the story. Probably not—after all, nobody would ever believe that he'd made a *great catch*. Louis wasn't even sure that *he* believed it.

"Hey, kid," a loud voice said.

Louis warily turned his head toward the field. A short, stout teenager with a dark tan was leaning into the stands. He was wearing a Yankee uniform without a number, which meant that he was a batboy.

"Me?" Louis asked, confused.

The batboy nodded. "They want to see you in the clubhouse."

"Am I in trouble?"

"Nah," the batboy said. "I think Mr. Maris just wants to say hi."

Louis's father had turned away from Mr. Evans in time to catch the end of the conversation, and Louis gave him a pleading glance. "Can I go, Dad?"

His father looked at Mr. Evans, who smiled a sympathetic smile.

"I know my son would never forgive me if I didn't let him meet Clemente," Mr. Evans said.

"Go," Louis's father said. "But don't take too long."

Louis handed the ball to his father for safekeeping, and

a moment later he slipped over the barrier separating the stands from the field. The batboy had already started toward the dugout, and as Louis took a few quick steps to catch him, he glanced furtively at the nearest security guard. It seemed impossible that he was walking across the infield at Yankee Stadium and nobody was trying to stop him. The grass felt soft and spongy under his feet, and from this angle the outfield appeared impossibly big. The crowd had already dissolved and the stands looked like a skeleton, just thin bones of steel and concrete without the covering flesh of the fans. Louis wanted to pause and take a picture with his brain, but he had to hustle to keep pace with the batboy as they slipped into the dugout. Everything in the dugout was painted Yankee blue—the steel girders and concrete walls and even the wood bat rack.

"Don't bother anyone," the batboy said as they ducked into a concrete tunnel. "And speak only if someone asks you a question."

They emerged into the locker room, and suddenly Louis was surrounded by faces that he knew intimately from his baseball cards. Yogi Berra was walking into the shower wearing only a towel. Elston Howard was buttoning his shirt. Bobby Richardson was combing his hair. Louis froze, disoriented by seeing the players without their uniforms. They looked like normal men doing normal things—although a few clusters of reporters in suits and sport jackets were a reminder that this wasn't just a locker room at the local YMCA. Louis took a slow breath, trying to calm his pounding heart. The room smelled like Ben-Gay and aftershave and sweat.

"Over here," the batboy said.

Roger Maris was perched on a stool, his hands clasped behind his head and his feet propped up on the wood frame of his large locker. The hair on the side of his head was cut as short as a Marine's, which made his ears look big. When he saw Louis, he swung his feet down and extended a huge palm.

"You must be that kid who caught that foul and gave me a second chance," he said.

Louis took the huge hand and nodded as they shook, his eyes focused on Roger's feet. He had removed his stirrups, and his white socks were dirty around the ankles.

"That was a good catch," Roger said. "I'd be proud of a catch like that."

Louis tried to say thank you, but the words died in a frightened mumble on his lips. He felt a hand on his back and he glanced up and suddenly found himself staring into the blazing blue eyes of Mickey Mantle. He was wearing just a T-shirt and uniform pants, and his forearms, which were covered by a thick carpet of blond hair, were as thick as Louis's thighs.

"Hey, kid," Mickey said. "Cat got your tongue?"

Louis managed to nod. Mickey smiled and glanced at Roger.

"Don't worry," Mickey said. "That big animal bites only every third kid who walks into this locker room."

"Yes, sir."

Mickey's smile got a little wider. "But I'm pretty sure the second kid just left."

He winked and turned back to his locker. Part of Louis wanted to slink back outside, back to the safety of a world where players were just photographs and numbers, but he knew that he would hate himself later if he let his nerves get the best of him.

"Don't mind Mickey," Roger said. "He likes to have fun with people."

Louis nodded again. His vocal cords felt as if they were covered in ice. Roger leaned forward, his voice dropping.

"I met Bronko Nagurski when I was about your age," he said. "You know who he is?"

"He was a football player and a wrestler."

"That's right. I just about keeled over when I shook his hand, but he gave me some good advice. He said it don't matter how big or small or young or old we are . . . everyone on this planet breathes the same air and sweats under the same sun. You understand what he meant?"

"Yes, sir," Louis said. He pulled his lineup card from his pocket, his hands shaking so much that the card was flapping like a fan. "Would you sign this, Mr. Maris?"

Roger nodded. "Sure thing."

He stood to reach into a cubbyhole and pulled a pen from between a can of deodorant and a canister of foot powder. Louis took the opportunity to peek past him. The locker had chain-link sides and wooden shelves, and it was about four feet wide and three feet deep—more of an open closet than a locker. A few towels and athletic supporters were draped over hooks, a hatbox rested next to a mitt on the top shelf, and a dark suit was neatly hung in the back corner. As Roger turned back around, Louis's eyes flashed to the concrete floor.

"You filled this out like a real pro," Roger said as he signed the card.

"I like numbers," Louis said.

Mickey turned around from his locker, a smile again on his face. "Oh, yeah?" he said in his slight drawl. "What am I hitting, kid?"

"After today?"

Mickey and Roger laughed, but Louis didn't know why it was funny.

"Sure," Mickey said. "After today."

".320."

Mickey was still smiling, and Louis got the sense that he was being teased. "Heck, that one was easy," Mickey said. "You've probably got it on your scorecard. Here's a better one. . . . What'd I hit in 1956?"

"That's easy too," Louis said. ".356 with fifty-two home runs and a hundred and thirty RBIs. You won the Triple Crown."

Tony Kubek, wearing only a towel, was walking past the little group, and Mickey turned and punched him on the shoulder.

"Hey," he said. "This kid knows all my stats."

Tony stared down at Louis. "Of course he knows your stats. You're Mickey Mantle and this is New York. Ask him if he knows what I hit last year."

Mickey turned back to Louis, one blond eyebrow raised. His face was as rubbery as a cartoon character's. Louis squinted as he tried to picture the numbers.

".273 with fourteen home runs and sixty-two RBIs," he said after a second.

Tony's mouth fell open. "How'd you know that, kid?"

Louis shrugged. "It says it on your baseball card."

"What else does it say?"

"Born in Milwaukee, Wisconsin. Full name is Anthony Christopher Kubek."

Mickey elbowed Tony in the ribs. "This kid's got a brain like a bear trap."

"Hey, Mick," Roger said. "I figure any kid who knows this much about baseball ought to be a batboy. What do you think?"

Mickey looked at Louis as if he were examining a bat for a crack, his mouth a tight line. And then he slowly nodded. "I figure you're right, Rog."

"Wait here," Maris said, with a small smile at Louis.

As Roger ambled across the crowded locker room and disappeared behind a wood door, Louis's breath started to come as heavily as if he had just run a sprint. A batboy? Is that what Roger had said? Louis wanted to ask someone to make sure, but Mickey had sunk into a conversation with Tony, and there was no way Louis was going to bother the starting shortstop and center fielder of the New York Yankees, not even if his hair spontaneously caught on fire.

Just when Louis felt as if he might collapse, Roger and Ralph Houk, the Yankees' manager, emerged from behind the wood door. Mr. Houk was still wearing his uniform and perfectly polished black shoes, and as they came across the room, Louis noticed that he walked with his back as stiff as a soldier's.

"This is the kid," Roger said when they reached Louis.

Mr. Houk carefully looked Louis up and down. His face was stern and his jaw was tightly clenched, but he had kind eyes.

"He's too young," Mr. Houk said. He must have noticed the expression on Louis's face because he quickly added, "Maybe in a year or two."

Mantle turned away from his conversation with Tony.

"Come on, skip," he said. "Give the kid a chance."

"Ask him a question about baseball," Roger said.

Mr. Houk folded his arms across his pinstriped jersey. Louis did his best to stand up straight—his stepmother always told him that he had a "deplorable slouch."

"Okay," Mr. Houk said after a long moment. "Here's an old baseball puzzle. There's a man on first and a man on second, no outs. How can a team turn a triple play without a baseball ever touching a fielder?"

"That's unfair," Mickey said. "There's no way I could answer that."

"Me neither," Roger said.

Louis closed his eyes. Sometimes he did the same thing in school when a teacher called him to the blackboard—it was easier to concentrate when you could pretend that it was just you and the question.

"No fielder can touch the ball," he repeated.

"That's right," Mr. Houk said. "Three outs."

The question seemed impossible, but Louis knew that Mr. Houk wouldn't ask it if there wasn't an answer. But how could you make an out without a fielder catching or throwing the ball? Maybe . . .

"It has to start with the umpire calling an infield fly," Louis said, thinking aloud.

"Correct," Mr. Houk said. "One out."

Okay, Louis thought to himself. The batter is out. How can the runners on base make an out without being tagged or forced? What was that mistake he'd made the previous spring in Little League? The one that had made his coach call him a "doofus" and launched yet another insulting nickname?

"Maybe the man on first runs past the man on second and is automatically out."

"That's two," Mr. Houk said.

Good, Louis thought. But now there was just one man on the base paths. What could one runner alone on the bases do to get called out? Louis racked his brain, trying to think of all the games he'd seen, all of the articles that he'd read in the paper. And just when he felt the players around him start to shift, just when he knew that Mr. Houk was going to say something and this incredible opportunity was going to disappear forever, Louis remembered an unusual play from a Boston-Baltimore game two years earlier.

"Oh," Louis said, his eyes popping open. "The last runner kicks the ball, and the umpire calls him out for interference."

Mr. Houk unfolded his arms. "That's three," he said.

"Attaboy," Roger said.

He and Mickey were smiling. Mr. Houk waved at the batboy who had brought Louis down to the locker room.

"Gabe!" he called.

Gabe dashed across the room, sliding to a halt on the polished floor in front of Mr. Houk. "Yes, sir."

Mr. Houk clapped Louis on the back. "This young gentleman knows more about baseball than most of the knuckleheads in this locker room, so we're going to have to make him a probationary batboy."

Gabe nodded. "Sure thing, Mr. Houk. I'll find him a uniform."

Mr. Houk turned his friendly eyes down toward Louis. "It's just a trial," he said. "But Gabe started on probation and he's been here for three years."

Louis closed his eyes again and took a deep breath. It had all happened so fast—ten minutes ago he had been getting ready to go home with his father, and now he had met Mickey and Roger and was going to be wearing a Yankee uniform for at least one day.

"I'll do my best," he said as his eyes opened.

But Mr. Houk was already gone.

CHAPTER TWO

Bottom of the First

Louis and his father returned to White Plains on the 6:45 p.m. train. The town was already quiet, and as they walked through the empty parking lot to the car and drove through the deserted streets, Louis wished that it was the middle of the day. He wanted to show someone—anyone—the ball. He wanted to find one of the stickball players and describe the catch. He wanted to tell the story of how he had actually spoken to Mickey Mantle and Roger Maris—and, best of all, how Mr. Houk had asked him, Louis May, to be a batboy for the New York Yankees.

But instead Louis was alone with his father, and as the car pulled up the driveway, Louis tried to find his courage. Louis hadn't mentioned his amazing chance to be a batboy, mostly because he was sure that his father would say no. He would probably give a long list of reasons: Louis's age, school starting in a few months, what Louis's mother and stepmother might say. And Louis would have to nod his head and swallow his disappointment and pretend that Mr. Houk had never made his incredible offer.

"Dad," Louis said as the car stopped at the top of the driveway.

Louis's voice sounded small even to him. His father must have sensed something was wrong because he turned in his seat, the keys dangling from his hand. Louis stared at the dashboard.

"There's something I have to tell you and it's really important and I know you'll want to say no but—"

"What is it, Louis?"

"They want me to be a batboy."

"Who? The Yankees?"

Louis nodded and managed to pry his eyes away from the dashboard. His father was smiling, but as Louis caught his eye his expression changed. Louis knew that look—it meant *no promises.*

"That's great," his father said. "We'll talk about it in the morning."

As Louis climbed out of the car, he tried to comfort himself with the fact that his father hadn't said no. There was still hope. But Louis also knew that "we'll talk about it in the morning" really meant "we'll talk about it after I've asked your stepmother." And very few conversations with Louis's stepmother went the way that Louis wanted them to go.

Louis went upstairs and brushed his teeth before tiptoeing into the bedroom that he shared with Bryce. The moon was almost full, and the light was streaming through the window. Louis was tucking his baseball mitt into the box at the foot of his bed when Bryce sat up and peered at him, his eyes just dark shadows.

"Why'd you bring your glove to the game?" he asked. "You can't catch."

Louis reached into the webbing of the mitt, pulled out the ball, and held it up. The leather looked ghostly in the moonlight.

"No way," Bryce said. "Your dad bought that."

Louis just smiled. Bryce flopped backward on his bed, and a few seconds later he began to make the faint snores he produced when he was pretending to be asleep. Louis tucked the glove into his trunk, took off his clothes, and slipped beneath his sheets. He was still clutching the ball, and he gently ran his hand back and forth across the laces. The rough feeling on his fingertips was a reminder that he hadn't just imagined the catch or being in the clubhouse. It was a reminder that he really had met Mickey Mantle and Roger Maris. And it was a reminder that if his father would just say yes, he would be able to go back to that locker room—and this time he would be able to put on a Yankee uniform.

Louis awoke the next morning to the muffled sound of his father's and stepmother's voices. He lay in bed for a minute or two before sliding out of bed, carefully opening the door of his room and creeping to the top of the stairs. Louis didn't consider himself a sneaky kid—he generally didn't eavesdrop or spy on people—but if this conversation was about his chance to become a batboy, he had to hear it.

"Why do they want him to be a batman?" his stepmother asked as Louis settled beside the wooden banister. They were in the kitchen, and her voice carried clearly up the stairs.

"Bat*boy*," Louis's father said. "I don't know, exactly. But I think it had something to do with the ball he caught."

"If anyone should be a batkid, it's Bryce. He's actually good at baseball."

"Louis loves baseball. He can quote more statistics than any adult I know."

"How's he going to get to the games?"

"He can take the train," Louis's father said. "And I'll pick him up at the station at night."

"I worry about Louis on that train. Who knows what kind of people are coming out of New York after a ball game?" She paused. "And what's he going to do when school starts in the fall? It's hard enough to make the transition to a new school without being at baseball games all the time."

"That's fair."

"I just think it would be a better fit for Bryce," his stepmother said after another pause. "He needs more men in his life. I know he misses his father."

"I'm his father."

"You know what I mean."

"I'm sure that Louis misses his mother, too. That's not the point."

"She can come out from the city anytime she wants. But Bryce will never get to see his father again and—"

She continued talking, but Louis didn't want to hear any more. He slid away from the banister, and when he closed the door to his room the steady drone of his stepmother's voice was reduced to a distant mumble. Bryce was still asleep—his breath was quiet and steady, unlike his fake snore—and Louis climbed into bed. He tried to force himself to relax, but his brain kept returning to the argument downstairs.

As far as Louis could tell, his father always won his arguments with Louis's mother and always lost his arguments with Louis's stepmother. It was at moments like this when Louis missed his mother the most. She didn't know anything about baseball, but she would have been excited about the catch. She wouldn't pretend that Bryce was the only kid in the world or make Louis play stickball or get in the way of his chance to be a batboy or—

Louis swung his feet out of bed. Usually when he started thinking about that kind of stuff he'd end up crying, and if Bryce heard him cry he'd call him a baby. And maybe Bryce was right. Would a batboy for the New York Yankees lie in bed feeling sorry for himself? No . . . a real batboy would go down to the kitchen and ask for what he wanted. That's what a real batboy would do.

Louis pulled on a pair of jeans and a T-shirt. As he padded down the stairs, his father and stepmother were still talking, but the voices stopped as he pushed his way through the kitchen door. They were sitting at the oak table, coffee mugs in front of them.

"Good morning," his father said with a smile. "Sleep well?"

Louis stayed next to the door. "I want to be a batboy."

"We know," his father said, his smile disappearing.

Louis's next words came in a rush. "It's a great opportunity and I'll get myself to the stadium and you don't have to worry about school because I can do homework at recess and when the Yankees are out of town. And I'll do extra chores around the house as soon as the season is over."

The pause after his words probably only lasted a few seconds, but it felt like an hour. His father was just watching him. Louis couldn't bring himself to look at his stepmother, but he was pretty sure that her eyes were narrow—the way they got when she was really mad.

"Okay," his father finally said. "You can be a batboy. But if your grades start to slip or you make trouble for your stepmother . . ."

Louis felt his cheeks tighten and knew that he must be smiling like an idiot. He wanted to go over and hug his father, but he also thought that he should leave the kitchen before his stepmother said anything or his father changed his mind. And so Louis just nodded his head and pushed his way back through the swinging door, and it was only when he was alone in the living room that a small *whoop* escaped from his lips and his fist instinctively punched the air.

CHAPTER THREE

Top of the Second

"**R**emember, it's only a tryout."

Louis was standing in a corner of the deserted Yankee clubhouse. Gabe was leaning against the tiny locker that the batboys shared, his thumbs shoved into the thick leather belt of his uniform. He had just finished reciting a baffling list of rules—most of which Louis had already forgotten—and now he was examining Louis with a skeptical eye.

"The only way to stay here is to work hard," Gabe said. "Just keep out of the way and follow orders. Got it?"

"Yeah," Louis said.

Gabe stepped away from the locker and waved his hand at a neatly folded uniform. "The manager expects you in his office in five minutes."

As Gabe crossed the room and disappeared into the tunnel that led to the field, Louis reached into the locker and carefully lifted the jersey. The wool felt heavy and rough against his hands. It looked exactly like a smaller version of the players' jerseys, except it had no number on the back.

Louis pulled his shirt off as fast as possible and then slipped the jersey over his bare chest and buttoned it with trembling fingers. The pants were too big for his skinny waist, but he cinched them up with the thick leather belt. He paused for a moment to figure out the stirrups—his Little League team had just used long socks—but a minute later he was fully dressed. Louis glanced around the clubhouse, suddenly nervous. He felt like an imposter in the uniform, and he half-expected the few players scattered around the room to give him dirty looks. But nobody seemed to notice him at all.

The manager's office was down a hallway on the far side of the clubhouse. Mr. Houk was on the phone, and Louis waited next to the door, trying not to fiddle—his step-mother said it was distracting when he fiddled. At last Mr. Houk hung up the phone. He was already wearing his uniform, and his dark hair was combed straight back from his forehead.

"You've returned," he said as his bright blue eyes settled on Louis.

"Yes, sir."

"I know it's your first day," Mr. Houk said, "but I have a very important assignment for you. I need you to find the umpires and tell them that we need a container of curveballs."

"A container of curveballs?"

Mr. Houk nodded, his mouth a thin line. "Our pitchers have been getting pounded, kid. We need the curveballs. The umpires' room is down the hall, take a left. You can't miss it."

"Yes, sir," Louis said, knowing that he had been dismissed.

Louis almost fell as he spun on his heel—his leather shoes were slippery on the linoleum—and then he strode through the clubhouse and down the hall. The umpires' room was marked with a small plaque, and Louis gently knocked. A deep voice told him to enter, and he slowly opened the door. Four men were sitting on a bench in a room not much bigger than a closet. They were stripped to their underwear, their black uniforms hanging from hooks on the wall. The fattest umpire was carefully rubbing a baseball with a dirty rag. A jar of mud was squeezed between his knees, and Louis knew that he was taking the shine off the new balls. The mud was supposed to be special—not too dark and not too slick—and its source was one of baseball's greatest secrets. Louis had heard it was a river somewhere in Pennsylvania, but that was just a rumor.

"Sorry to bother you," Louis said. "But Mr. Houk said that he—the Yankees—need a container of curveballs."

The fat umpire glanced up from his work and raised an eyebrow. "He did, did he?"

"Yes, sir."

The fat umpire reached into a laundry bag of balls. He rustled around for a moment before withdrawing an empty hand. "I'm sorry, but we don't have any curveballs tonight. I'll try to find some for tomorrow."

"Okay," Louis said, trying to hide his disappointment. It was his very first assignment and he'd already failed.

"I'll tell you what we do need," the fat umpire said. He flicked his head at the umpire to his right. "Ralph here left the key to the batter's box out on the field last night. I know some of the boys are out taking batting practice. Would you ask them if they've seen it?"

"Yes, sir."

Louis carefully closed the door and then ran back down the hallway and out the tunnel onto the field. He caught a glimpse of the empty stands, but his attention was focused on home plate. Three or four players, including Mickey Mantle, were gathered around the mesh cage as Elston Howard took batting practice. Elston's swings looked lazy, but every time he made solid contact the ball would leap off his bat so fast that Louis would lose it for a second or two against the blue sky.

The players were laughing and joking amongst themselves, and Louis waited a dozen feet away, not quite sure what he should do. It was Mickey who finally turned around, and when he noticed Louis a broad smile spread across his freckled face.

"Hey, it's the walking baseball card," he said. "You got my updated statistics, kid?"

Louis shuffled a few steps closer. "The umpires wanted to know if you'd seen the key to the batter's box. They said they left it out here last night."

"The key to the batter's box?" Mickey wrinkled his forehead, one foot scuffing the dirt. After a moment he looked across the cage at Whitey Ford, the Yankees' best pitcher. "Hey, Whitey," he said. "You seen the key to the batter's box?"

Whitey shook his head, his fair blond hair—the reason for his nickname—gleaming in the sun. "Nope. But we're about to start taking infield, and I sure could use the left-handed fungo bat."

"Do you know what a fungo bat is?" Mickey asked Louis.

"No, sir."

"It's got a real thin handle so it's easier for a coach to hit flies to the outfield. Problem is, our coach is left-handed. And we've only got right-handed ones out here. You understand?"

"I'll go ask in the clubhouse," Louis said.

"That's a real good idea," Mickey said. "Ask Roger, if you can find him."

Louis turned and dashed back toward the clubhouse, but his feet slowed as he skipped down the dugout steps. He'd been so focused on his errands that he hadn't actually listened to the assignments, but now, as he repeated them in his head, he started to feel a little silly. By the time he entered the clubhouse, his dash had slowed almost to a crawl, and he finally stopped a yard or two away from Roger Maris's locker. Roger was tying his shoes.

"Hey, kid," he said. "Welcome back."

"Hello, Mr. Maris." Louis's cheeks felt as if they were on fire. "There's no such thing as a left-handed fungo bat, is there?"

Roger smiled a faint smile. "No. Lefty and righty bats are exactly the same."

"And the batter's box doesn't need a key because it's just a couple of lines in the dirt."

"That's right."

"And baseballs are the same too. They just curve because of the way you throw them."

"Well, some pitchers put grease or spit on the ball. But . . . yeah."

"Oh," Louis said.

He suddenly felt stupid, and he wondered what would happen if he just took off his uniform and slunk out of the clubhouse. What would his father say? And how would he feel in a week or a month when he realized that he had given up a chance to be a batboy for the Yankees? But maybe being a batboy wasn't worth it; Louis didn't need more people making fun of him or playing mean jokes on him. After all, he could get that playing stickball—or, if he waited a few months, at his new school.

The room got blurry, and Louis was just about to start running for the bathroom so he wouldn't embarrass himself when he felt a firm hand on his shoulder. It was Roger.

"Listen," Roger said. "The boys are just having fun with you. It happens in a clubhouse. You know why?"

Louis shook his head.

"Because a hundred sixty-two games a year is a whole lot of baseball. We've got to figure out ways to entertain ourselves, and one of those ways is pranks. I've gotten pies in my face, and hot feet, and pepper in my chewing gum, and all sorts of things. It's just what we do to keep from going crazy, I guess."

"Did you ever ask anyone for a bag of curveballs?"

"Nope. But a couple of years ago Gabe supposedly spent two hours looking for the key to the batter's box. He even asked Mr. Topping, the Yankees' owner, if he'd seen it."

Louis tried to picture the cool and collected Gabe running around on a wild-goose chase. "Really?"

"Really," Roger said. "Now you go tell Gabe that you're ready for a real job and see what he says, okay?"

Louis nodded and went to find Gabe. From that moment until the end of the game he was so busy that he never had time to be nervous. Before the first pitch he filled the water coolers, folded towels, and made sure there were enough sunflower seeds and bubble gum for the players in the dugout. When the game started, he was responsible for shuttling messages to the clubhouse and running extra balls to the home plate umpire. It was a hot, muggy Sunday afternoon, and several times Louis had to refill the cooler of ice in the corner of the dugout.

The game itself was a rout. The Yankees hit five home runs and won 13-4. Maris had two of the homers and Mantle had one. When Roger hit his second home run in the seventh inning, he came over to Louis in the dugout and rubbed his head.

"I guess you're my good-luck charm," he said. "You better stick around."

The game ended close to five, and the players shook hands before retreating to the cool of the clubhouse. Gabe and Louis cleaned the dugout, and when they finally went inside, most of the players were in the shower. But a thick group of eager reporters had trapped Mickey and Roger at their lockers. Their home run binge over the last few days meant that Roger now had 30 home runs and Mickey had 28, which meant that Roger was on pace to break Babe Ruth's famous single-season home run record and Mickey was on pace to tie it.

Louis's last assignment was to clean and polish the players' cleats. He was in a deserted corner of the room near Kubek's locker, his arms filled with dirty leather shoes, when a short man in a dark suit cornered him. The man had a big bald spot in the middle of his head and was carrying a small notebook under one arm.

"You're new here," the man said. "Right?"

Louis nodded. He couldn't explain why, but something about the man made him uncomfortable.

"My name's Nathan Scully," the man said. "I write for the *Daily News*. Do you read my stuff?"

"No," Louis said. "I read the *Post* and the *Times*."

Nathan shrugged. "No big thing. Here's the deal, kid. Maris has got a big stack of fan mail in his locker. You wait for things to get quiet, then grab me a couple of letters. And I give you this."

Nathan reached into his pocket and pulled out a baseball card in a plastic sleeve. Louis caught a glimpse of Joe DiMaggio's face and big sloping letters written in a thick pen, and his hand instinctively reached toward the card.

"Is that really Joe's signature?" he asked.

Nathan held the card just out of reach.

"Yup," he said. "And all you gotta do is get a little mail. Lots of batboys do it."

Louis glanced at the crowd around Roger and then back at the card. The kids in the neighborhood would kill for a signed DiMaggio card—it might even be more valuable than a Babe Ruth. Bryce would probably trade a kidney for it.

Nathan was staring at him, one eyebrow raised. Every muscle in Louis's body wanted to reach out and take that card, but a little voice in the back of his head told him that it would be a decision he would regret.

"No thanks," Louis said.

Louis clutched the cleats to his chest and scurried toward the cleaning supplies in the far corner of the room. When he risked a glance back toward Kubek's locker, the reporter had disappeared. Louis wasn't sure what he should do.

The safest decision would be to pretend that the conversation had never happened, but what if the reporter was approaching other batboys? What if he was stealing things from lockers on his own? Shouldn't someone know that a snake was loose in the clubhouse?

After five minutes of fierce internal debate Louis finally walked down the hall to the manager's office. This time Mr. Houk was wearing just a T-shirt and his uniform pants as he shuffled through a sheaf of papers on his desk. Louis knocked on the wall next to the door, and Mr. Houk glanced up at him.

"I guess you never found those curveballs." He said it with a smile, but it was a friendly smile instead of a mocking smile, and Louis felt his courage grow.

"I don't want to be a tattletale," he said, "but a man just asked me to do something and I don't think it was right."

Mr. Houk slowly stood up, walked around his desk, and closed the door.

"Sit," he said, pointing at a metal chair. As Louis perched on the edge of the seat, Mr. Houk leaned back against the desk, his arms folded. "Tell me what happened."

"I was in the clubhouse, and a reporter named Nathan Scully offered me a DiMaggio-signed baseball card to steal mail from Mr. Maris's locker."

Mr. Houk's face got bright red, and for a moment Louis was worried that he was about to start yelling. But instead he took a long, slow breath, and when he spoke, his voice was calm.

"You were right to come to me," he said. "You see, Louis, there's a difference between being a fan and being in a clubhouse. Some of the things that happen in here don't have much to do with baseball. But that's just the way it is."

"Why did that man want the mail?" Louis asked.

"Who knows? Maybe for some article he's going to print about how Roger doesn't respect his fans. Maybe it was something else. You can't control that, Louis. All you can control is yourself, and you did a good job today."

"Thank you, sir."

Mr. Houk opened the door to his office, and Louis stood.

"You come to me if Nathan Scully talks to you again," he said. "And Louis . . . consider yourself a full-time batboy."

"Thank you, sir," Louis said, trying to contain his smile.

Mr. Houk shook his head. "Don't thank me," he said. "You're the one who was honest enough to turn down Scully's offer and brave enough to tell me what happened. And I'll tell you something, son. I've spent a lot of time in baseball and a lot of time in the Army. And in both places we always needed all the brave, honest men we could get."

CHAPTER FOUR

Bottom of the Second

Louis awakened the next morning to the sound of something clumping against the floor of the bedroom. He sat up and rubbed his eyes. Bryce was in the closet, his back to the room, and as Louis watched, a pair of black shoes came flying over Bryce's shoulder and landed on the carpet with a *thump*. Louis leaned over the edge of the bed to get a closer look at the shoes. They were the black leather ones that his dad made him wear to school.

"What are you doing?" Louis asked.

Bryce emerged from the closet, his hands on his hips. "Your stuff was touching my side."

"Can't you just move it over?"

"I'm tired of moving it over."

He tossed one last object—a belt—onto the rug and then stalked over to the door. As Louis let his head fall back onto the pillow, Bryce's voice cut across the room.

"You know, the Yankees aren't going to let you be a

batboy anymore once they figure out how bad you are at baseball."

Louis snapped upright again and glanced at the door, but Bryce was already gone. Although Louis lay in bed for a few more minutes, he knew that he wouldn't be able to fall back asleep—not after Bryce's last comment—so eventually he got up, shoved everything back onto his side of the closet, and began rearranging his baseball cards. He had always kept his collection sorted by year, but recently it had occurred to him that it might be smarter to organize the players by their teams. That way he could find all of a player's statistics as quickly as possible, which would help if anyone decided to quiz him again.

As Louis was coming downstairs for lunch, the phone rang. Louis missed the first part of the conversation, but as he settled into his chair at the kitchen table, he heard his stepmother say, "You know, you really should give us more warning."

She seemed annoyed, and Louis tried to ignore the rest of the call and keep his eyes on his peanut butter and jelly sandwich. When she hung up, she sat at the table and carefully unfolded her napkin before looking at Louis.

"That was your mother," she said. "She's coming out from the city tonight to take you to dinner."

"Oh," Louis mumbled. His mouth was sticky with peanut butter.

"She'll be here at six. You need to do those chores this afternoon, but I want you showered and presentable by five thirty. Okay?"

Louis nodded. Ever since he could remember he had helped his father with four chores on Sunday afternoon.

Louis's mother used to tease his father about why it always had to be four, and his father would always give the same answer: "Because five is too many and three is too few." But the previous Sunday Louis had been at the Yankees game, so his father had done his chores alone.

He had therefore left a list for Louis before he went to work on Monday—four chores, of course—and after lunch Louis put on his work shirt and went outside. He raked clippings from the lawn, yanked weeds out of the flower garden, dragged the trash to the bin behind the house, and painted a small table that his stepmother had found at a rummage sale. Bryce hated chores and would usually weasel his way out of doing them, but Louis didn't mind. It felt good to look at a freshly cut lawn or a table still wet with paint and remember how raggedy they had been just an hour earlier.

Louis's favorite part of Sunday chores, however, was the end. His father would open two bottles of Coke, and they would sit together on the steps of the front porch. Louis would try not to drink his soda too fast, because when he drank too fast he got a stomachache, and his father would dab at his sweaty forehead with his shirt. They never said much, but Louis liked the silence. And it was the only time in the week when Louis knew that he and his father would be together without his stepmother or Bryce.

But this afternoon Louis was alone, so when he was finished, he skipped the Coke and trudged upstairs to take a shower. When he emerged from the bathroom, his stepmother was standing outside to check that he had cleaned behind his ears—her test of a thorough scrubbing—and then Louis put on a school shirt and khaki pants and tried to slick down his unruly hair. It was as thick and stubborn as the bristles of a brush, and when it got too long it would stick out in a brown plume from the back of his head. His mother used to call the plume his "rooster tail."

"She's going to meet you at Garibaldi's," his stepmother said when Louis came downstairs. "Make sure that you look both ways before crossing Main Street."

Garibaldi's was a popular pizza place. They served Louis's favorite drink, a "brown cow," which was a root beer float with vanilla ice cream and a splash of chocolate syrup. Louis usually liked going to Garibaldi's, but today he was a little nervous. Local kids were always at the restaurant, and back in his old town every time kids from school saw his mother, Louis would hear about it on the playground or ball field the next day.

When Louis got to the restaurant, his mother was already sitting at a booth in the back. As she gave him a big hug, Louis tried to pretend that nobody was staring at them. All of the other women in Garibaldi's were wearing nice dresses and fancy jewelry and had hair that looked like plastic. But Louis's mother was wearing a thick wool sweater, canvas pants that were rolled up at the bottom, and a necklace that appeared to be made from driftwood. Her long, straight hair flowed all the way to the small of her back.

"So tell me about your summer," she said when they were settled. "What have you been doing?"

"Nothing much."

"You must have something exciting to tell me," she said. "Something about snakes or snails or puppy dog tails."

Louis stared down at the plastic checkered tablecloth.

"Well . . . I went to a Yankees game and caught a ball and now they want me to be a batboy."

"Oh, Louis. That's wonderful. You must be thrilled."

Louis glanced up. His mother was watching him, a smile on her face. She didn't know anything about baseball—she probably couldn't name a single player on the Yankees—but she was still glowing. This was why it was so hard for Louis to stay angry with her. Sometimes, when he was lying in bed at night, Louis would get mad that she had divorced his father and moved to New York City and that she broke so many promises. And sometimes Louis would even swear to himself that he wouldn't just forgive her for everything the moment she showed that she cared about him, but those promises always vaporized when they were actually together.

"I was thinking," Louis said slowly. "Maybe . . ."

"Maybe what?"

"Maybe since I'm going to be in the city for games, I could stay with you. Just sometimes."

There was a long pause. Louis felt as if his eyes were boring a hole in the tablecloth.

"I'd love that," his mother finally said. "But we'll have to ask your father."

"I know another kid whose parents are divorced, and he lives with his mom."

"Everybody's different, Louis."

Louis felt a surge of frustration. His mother often said vague things like that as if they were answers, but they weren't. Of course everyone was different—what Louis wanted to know was *why* his family had to be different. Why his mother had moved to New York and only saw him once a month. Why he had to live in White Plains and go to a new school and make new friends and live with his stepmother and Bryce. Why nobody would ever give him a real answer to anything.

"I don't understand," he finally said. "Is it because you don't care about me?"

"No, baby," she said, her voice raspy. "That's not it. I love you and I miss you. But your father and I think it's best for you to live out here. Have a normal life with a father and a stepmother. We want you to be happy, Louis."

Her hands had covered his on the table, and the edges of her eyes were wet. Louis did his best to smile.

"It's okay," he said. "I am happy."

They split a medium pizza. His mother ordered green peppers and mushrooms on her half, and Louis had pepperoni. After dinner she walked him back to the house. Louis's father was smoking his pipe in the rocking chair on the porch— he wasn't allowed to smoke inside—and he waved as they came through the gate. Usually Louis's mother would just wave back and leave, but today she followed Louis up the creaky wood steps.

"Hello, Phil," she said.

"Hello, Jean," he said.

"Louis just told me about the Yankees," she said, her tone unusually formal. "We were thinking that since he's going to be in the city anyway, he should come visit me for a weekend or two."

Louis's father took a long puff on his pipe. "I don't know."

"It would be good for him to see the city."

Smoke emerged from his mouth in a rollicking gust. "I don't know why this is so hard to understand, Jean. I don't want my son hanging around those delinquents, beatniks, and coffee drinkers."

His mother raised an eyebrow. "It would be good for Louis if you had more of an open mind."

"We'll talk about this later," he said in his stern voice.

Louis's mother stared at him for a long moment before turning and kissing Louis on the forehead.

"You stay sweet," she said.

Louis watched as his mother walked back across the lawn to the sidewalk, her long hair swaying back and forth like a thick, brown snake. When she disappeared down the block, he turned and went into the living room. His favorite show, *The Rifleman*, was about to start on ABC. Most of the kids at school preferred another Western called *Bonanza*, which was an hour-long show in color on Sunday night, but Louis liked the simplicity of *The Rifleman*. It was about a man and his son who lived on a homestead on the frontier. The man used his special repeating rifle to fight for justice, but he also spent a lot of the show teaching his son how to live in the wild.

The episode ended at nine and Louis went upstairs. Bryce was lying on his bed reading an issue of *MAD* magazine, but when he noticed Louis, he rolled over so his back was facing the room. Bryce was always angry when Louis came home from dinner with his mother. Maybe it was because his own dad had died in Korea, or maybe it was just because he wanted to go out for pizza. Either way, Louis knew that it would be a waste of time to try to talk with him.

As Louis brushed his teeth, he wondered what it would

be like to have a father who had died in a war. Sometimes, when Louis was feeling sorry for himself, he thought that it would almost be easier if his own mother was dead. He wouldn't have to spend so much time wishing that she was in the house or wondering when he was going to see her again. But Louis knew that he was wrong. Maybe someday his mother would move to White Plains, or maybe he would get to visit her more often, but dead was forever. And that was much worse.

CHAPTER FIVE

Top of the Third

Roger Maris hit two more home runs in the next three games, which meant that he was now on pace to hit 67 and shatter Babe Ruth's single-season record of 60. When he got back to the dugout after the second home run, he rubbed Louis's head.

"You really are my good-luck charm," he said. "From now on I'm calling you 'Lucky.'"

The Yankees played Cleveland the next night, and Louis arrived at the ballpark in the mid-afternoon. He had just finished returning the players' cleats to their lockers when Roger emerged from the trainer's room wearing his uniform pants and a T-shirt. He was rubbing his shoulder.

"Hey, Lucky," he said. "Play catch with me for a minute."

"On the field?" Louis asked, his stomach tightening.

Roger looked at him strangely. "Yeah, on the field."

"I don't have a glove," Louis said.

Roger walked to his locker, pulled out a glove, and tossed it across the room. It landed at Louis's feet, and he picked it up and slid it over his hand. The leather was so worn that it felt floppy on his fingers.

"Be careful with that one," Roger said. "I need that glove."

Louis glanced around the locker room. "Are you sure you don't want to play catch with someone else?"

"What's the matter?" Roger asked. "You like baseball, but you don't want to play catch?"

Louis stared at the floor. "I've got a rag arm."

Roger shrugged. "We'll take it real easy, okay? I've just gotta stretch my shoulder. I slept on it funny."

There were still two hours until the game, and the stadium was almost empty. Bill Stafford, the Yankees starting pitcher, was stretching near second base, and a few fans were scattered in the stands. Roger went out to his usual position in right field and Louis stood near the foul line, about forty feet away. Roger tossed the ball to Louis, his throwing motion lazy and exaggerated, but the ball still snapped out of his hand and popped into Louis's glove.

As Louis slowly turned the ball in his hand, he tried to remember everything his Little League coach had ever taught him. He focused on Roger's glove, pulled his arm back like a catapult, took a firm step forward, and let his fingers slide off the stitches. The ball flew about twenty feet and landed between them. It bounced several times in the close-cropped grass before slowly rolling to a stop near Roger's feet.

"Don't think," Roger said. "Just throw."

He tossed the ball back, and this time Louis snatched the

ball out of his glove and hurled it as quickly as possible. Roger had to take a step to his left, but he caught it at chest level.

"Good," he said.

They played catch for ten or fifteen minutes. Louis bounced a few, but generally he did okay. At the very end he noticed a few kids in the first row of the right-field stands. They were clutching pens and autograph pads, and Louis could feel their jealous glares even when he wasn't looking at them. His last few throws skittered in the grass, and he heard mocking laughter.

"Who said you have a rag arm?" Roger asked as they walked back to the dugout.

"Some kids at my old school," Louis said. "And my Little League coach."

Roger shook his head. "Your arm is fine. But did you notice what happened when you started looking at those kids?"

"It's hard. With people watching."

"It happens to everyone." They had reached the dugout, and Roger stopped and waved at the vast blue stands. "Usually I try to pretend that the crowd is just a big ocean. The cheers are the sounds of the waves or something. But every now and then I look in the stands, and one person is looking back at me, and suddenly I realize that the crowd is really thousands and thousands of people. Booing me. Cheering me. Praying that I get a hit. Hoping I strike out. You know what happens then?"

"What?" Louis asked.

"My throat gets real tight and my palms get real sweaty, and I drop the ball or throw to the wrong man. Because my brain starts to get in the way. You understand?"

Louis nodded and Roger patted him on the shoulder.

"Thanks for the catch," he said. "Let's go get ready."

The game was against the Indians, who were in third place, six games behind the Yankees. In the bottom of the fourth, with one out and the game tied 0-0, Roger hit a sharp single to right field. Mickey was up next, and he took a huge swing at the first pitch. As the ball skittered foul, Louis heard the telltale dead crack of a broken bat. Gabe was responsible for the bats, but as Louis glanced down the dugout toward the rack, he remembered that Gabe had just run into the clubhouse to go to the bathroom.

Louis sidled down the dugout, not quite sure what to do. Fortunately, Buck Cooper, the assistant equipment manager, noticed the situation. He turned to the rack, pulled out a bat, and shoved it at Louis.

"Be quick," he said. "Mick doesn't like to wait."

Louis turned and sprinted onto the field. Mickey was standing by the umpire, the broken bat at his feet. Louis handed him the new bat, collected the shards of broken ash, and then dashed back to the dugout. Roger was right— it was scary to be on the field when the stands were full. The noise surrounded you, a strange, clamoring echo, and it felt as if thousands of eyes were creeping along your skin.

Just as Louis slipped back into the dugout, the pitcher started his windup. Mickey took another vicious cut, but this time the ball stayed fair and skipped to the shortstop. The ball whipped from second to first for a double play. Mickey tried to beat it out, but after he passed first base he turned and jogged back to his abandoned bat. He picked it up and stared fixedly at it as he walked to the bench.

"This is the wrong darn bat," he said to nobody in particular. "This is Bobby's bat."

Louis glanced at Buck Cooper, but he was staring at the floor of the dugout, his face blank.

"Hey, kid," Mickey said. "You gave me the wrong bat."

"I'm sorry," Louis said.

Mickey shook his head. "Sorry don't pay the rent."

Roger came out of the dugout and slapped Mickey's glove into his hand. "Come on, Mick," he said. "You never care what bat you use. You hit a home run with my bat last year."

"I care when I ground into a double play," Mickey said with a long look at Louis.

He turned and jogged out to his position. Louis pulled his cap low over his eyes and slunk to the part of the bench in the farthest corner of the dugout. He felt sick to his stomach. When the other players heard about his mistake, nobody was ever going to let him touch a bat again. And, worse than that, he'd made Mickey Mantle ground into a double play. Mickey Mantle!

The inning had just started when Buck Cooper ambled down the dugout and settled next to Louis. His hair was black except for a little white streak on top. The players called him "Skunk."

"Listen," Buck said in a quiet voice. "I would have said something, but Mickey's got a real temper. You understand?"

"Yeah," Louis said.

"It's a long season," Buck said. "These things happen all the time. Just forget about it."

But Louis couldn't forget about it, not even after the

Yankees won the game 4-0. And as he tossed and turned in bed that night, he replayed the moment that he handed the bat to Mickey over and over again in his head. Maybe it wasn't his fault that Buck had picked out the wrong bat, but a good batboy would have double-checked. Gabe, for example, never would have made that mistake. Batboys were in the dugout to help the players, but Louis had made things worse. And that was unforgivable.

CHAPTER SIX

Bottom of the Third

The Yankees won three out of four games against Boston before the first All-Star break, which put them half a game behind Detroit in the race for the American League pennant. Six Yankees had been selected for the All-Star team, including Roger and Mickey, and Whitey Ford was the starting pitcher.

Louis planned on watching the game at home with his father, but at the last moment his stepmother asked Bryce to invite some kids who would be entering the seventh grade with Louis. Although Louis understood that she was trying to be nice, it was a typically stupid adult plan. Anyone who Bryce knew was likely to be popular and a good athlete—and, sure enough, the two kids he invited, Alex and Doug, were the best seventh graders from stickball. They spent the game ignoring Louis and joking with Bryce, who was probably closer to their age anyway.

Louis enjoyed the game itself. The National League won

5-4 on a single by Roberto Clemente in the bottom of the tenth inning. The game was played in San Francisco's Candlestick Park, and the wind was so vicious that Stu Miller, a reliever for the Giants, froze in his windup after being caught by a particularly vicious gust and was called for a balk.

After Clemente's winning hit, Louis's stepmother gave Bryce a dollar to treat the kids to ice cream. The parlor was five blocks away, and as they walked the tree-lined streets, Bryce, Alex, and Doug laughed and joked. Louis trailed behind them, still thinking about the game. It had been a rough outing for the Yankees' stars: Mickey had been hit-less, and Roger had gone 1 for 4 with two strikeouts.

They still were a few blocks from the store when Louis overheard raised voices. It sounded like the beginning of an argument, and he took a few steps to catch up.

"Bill Skowron's a first baseman," Bryce was saying. "He's gotta be huge."

Alex, a thick kid with skin so white that it looked as if he'd been dipped in flour, shook his head. "I'm telling you. Kubek's taller than him."

"There's no way a shortstop is taller than a guy called Moose," Bryce said.

"Kubek is four inches taller than Moose," Louis said. Everyone turned to look at him, and he swallowed hard. "Well, at least three."

Doug rolled his eyes. He had curly dark hair, and his mouth always turned down slightly at the corners. "That's dumb. Kubek's a shortstop, and shortstops are always short. It's in the name!"

If it had been any subject other than baseball and the Yankees, Louis would have kept his mouth shut. But he knew that he was right. "Tony's the tallest guy on the team except for Rollie Sheldon and Jim Coates," he said.

"How do you know?" Doug asked.

"It's on their baseball cards."

"They lie on those cards."

Louis blinked. It had never occurred to him that anyone would doubt the numbers on a baseball card—that information was sacred.

"The cards are right," Louis finally said. "I've seen everyone on the team without shoes. I know how tall they are."

"When have you ever seen a baseball player without shoes?" Alex asked with a doubtful sneer.

"I'm a batboy. For the Yankees."

Louis had been inching his way closer and closer to the other three boys, but he instinctively took a big step away as everyone stared at him.

"That's a lie," Alex said.

His voice was loud and aggressive. Louis tried not to panic and looked at Bryce. "Tell them. It's true, right?"

Bryce stared back at Louis for what felt like an hour but was probably only a few seconds. "Yeah," he finally said. "He's a batboy."

Louis hadn't been exactly sure what kind of reaction he would get if he told kids about being a batboy, and the answer—at least with Doug and Alex—was stunned silence. Their mouths fell open and their eyes bulged out of their heads, and for a moment Louis wondered if a ghost had appeared on the sidewalk behind him. Doug was the first one to recover.

"What are they like?" he asked.

"The players?"

Doug nodded.

"Kind of normal. I mean, they can't always act normal with reporters, but when they're alone they tell jokes and play pranks and stuff."

"Do you get to walk on the field?"

"Before the game," Louis said. "It's really soft, like the nicest lawn in White Plains. And the dirt in the infield is so flat that you could roll a marble across it."

"What about Mickey?" Alex asked. "What's Mickey like?"

"He laughs a lot. And he likes to kid around with the other guys. Especially Whitey."

"Ask him who he likes better," Bryce said with a sidelong look at Louis. "Roger Maris or Mickey Mantle."

Doug and Alex looked at him, suddenly suspicious. Louis knew that he was in dangerous territory, but he couldn't bring himself to completely lie.

"I like them both," he said after a pause that had lasted a few seconds too long.

"My dad says that Roger Maris is a selfish hick," Doug said.

"He's been really nice to me. And the guys in the clubhouse like him."

"He sulks about his statistics," Alex said. "I read that in the paper."

Louis shook his head. "Some of the reporters hate him, so they make up stories."

"Remember when he had to come out of the game earlier this year because he'd gone to an eye doctor?" Bryce asked.

"The Yankees ordered him to go to the eye doctor," Louis said. "And they won the game anyway!"

Although Louis tried to keep his voice calm, he could

feel the conversation turning. Kids like Alex and Doug were like sharks, and once they smelled blood in the water, it wouldn't matter if Louis told a dozen stories about the Yankees' clubhouse. They would attack.

"All I know is that Mickey would never quit on his team like that," Bryce said.

"Roger didn't quit!" The words emerged almost as a shout, but Louis couldn't control himself. "They took him out of the game because he couldn't see."

Bryce smiled, a wicked glint in his eye. The blood was in the water. "If you like him so much, why don't you marry him?"

"Ooh, I'm Roger Maris," Alex said in a falsetto. "My eye hurts and I can't play."

Louis turned and started walking back toward the house. He heard a few catcalls and taunts behind him, but he tried to ignore them. He had messed up; if he had just been able to resist Bryce's bait, Alex and Doug would have remained focused on Louis being a batboy, and everything would have been okay. But instead he had lost control of his emotions, and now they'd make fun of Roger Maris every chance they got. Just to get under his skin.

When Louis got back to the house, his father was sitting on the porch in his usual spot, his pipe smoldering in his hand.

"I thought you were getting ice cream," he said.

Louis shrugged, and his father patted the wicker chair next to him. Louis crossed the porch and sat.

"What did you think of the game?" his father asked.

"It was okay," Louis said. "Too many errors."

"That wind was trouble." Louis was silent and his

father gave him a long look. "What's the matter?"

"I don't like it here," Louis said, the words rushing together. "You told me when we moved to White Plains that it would get better. But I've been here two months and it hasn't gotten better. The kids back in Teaneck liked baseball."

"The kids here like baseball," his father said. "Bryce and his friends play that stick game every day."

Louis shook his head. "It's different. In Teaneck, we liked the Yankees. The whole team. Here, they like some players and they hate some players, and I don't know why."

"It's because you're getting older, Louis. That's what people do when they get older. They get critical."

"Is that what happened with you and mom?"

His father smiled, a funny look in his eye. "Yeah, I guess you could say that."

"I want to visit her," Louis said.

In the long silence that followed, Louis knew that he had pushed his luck. When his father made up his mind, he didn't like to be challenged, and Louis had heard no wiggle room when his mother had asked if he could go and visit her in New York. Louis was therefore shocked when his father finally shrugged.

"Okay," he said. "You can go. But I want you to make me a promise."

"Anything."

"Maybe we've only been here for two months, but I feel like you haven't given this place a chance. Not the local kids, not Bryce, and certainly not your stepmother. So you can visit your mother, but I want you to promise that when you get back you'll try a little harder."

Louis felt his jaw clench. It wasn't fair of his father to say that he wasn't trying—he tried every day. He tried in those stupid stickball games. He tried to live by his stepmother's rules. And he tried with Bryce, even though Bryce had never been nice to him—not once.

"I am trying," he said after a few seconds, his voice cracking a little. "But nobody here likes me."

His father raised an eyebrow. "Louis, you walked into that Yankees' locker room and twenty minutes later you were a batboy. Because they liked you. All I want is for you to work that same magic here in White Plains. Okay?"

"Okay," Louis said.

But as he walked upstairs, Louis knew that he had just been humoring his father, because once kids turned on you, it was hopeless. Bryce had insured that Doug and Alex and probably everyone else in the stickball games would make fun of him every chance they got. And Louis could try as hard as he wanted, but that was just the way it was going to be.

CHAPTER SEVEN

Top of the Fourth

Early the next morning Louis took the train to Yankee Stadium to help pack the clubhouse. The team was leaving on a fourteen-game road trip that would keep them out of New York for almost two weeks, and the batboys and clubhouse attendants had to help load spare uniforms and cleats and other equipment into the huge trunks that would follow the team from city to city.

Roger and Mickey and the other All-Stars had flown directly from San Francisco to Chicago—the first stop on the road trip—but the rest of the team met at the stadium to catch a bus to the airport. The players began to arrive shortly before lunch. Louis was folding uniform socks in the trainer's room when he felt a firm hand on his shoulder. It was Bob Cerv, a reserve outfielder. Bob was wearing a plain black suit, and between his slight paunch and the thick lines around his eyes he looked more like a farmer in his Sunday finest than a ballplayer.

"Hiya, Lucky," he said. "Roger called. He needs a favor."

"What kind of favor?" Louis asked.

Bob settled onto one of the trainer's tables. "Well, we both need a favor, actually. See, Rog and Mick and me are room-mates up in Queens. Last night Rog calls in a panic from San Francisco because he bought a birthday present for his kid and forgot to put it in the mail. So I say, 'No problem. I'll take care of it.' But I get out of bed this morning and start packing and it just plumb slipped my mind."

"You didn't mail it?" Louis asked. Bob had a circular way of reaching the point that always left Louis a little dizzy.

"That's right," Bob said. "So I was hoping that you could run up to our apartment sometime today or tomorrow, grab that package out of Rog's room, and drop it by the post office."

"You want me to go to the apartment?" Louis asked, try-ing his best to sound nonchalant. He didn't want Bob to think that he was too eager, but it was hard to contain his excitement. How many kids got to see Mickey Mantle and Roger Maris's apartment?

"Yeah," Bob said. "It's up in Queens. I'll write down the address and give you the keys." Bob tugged his wallet out of his pocket and pulled out a few dollars. "Here's some money for the postage. And, Lucky . . ."

"Yeah?"

"No need to mention any of this to Rog, okay?"

"Sure thing," Louis said.

The players filed into their bus soon afterward. Louis did his best to help the clubhouse attendants carry the heavy trunks out to the trucks, and then he got back on a train to White Plains. The next morning he waited until his father had left for work to come downstairs for breakfast.

"I have to go to the stadium," he said as his stepmother poured his orange juice.

"Why?" she asked. "I thought the team was out of town for a week or two."

"They need more help packing."

"Are they paying you for this, Louis?"

"Nope," Louis said. "But Whitey Ford gave me a buck for carrying his bag last week."

She rolled her blue eyes toward the ceiling. "Child labor's supposed to be against the law."

"I'll be back before dinner."

"Fine," she said. "Just be careful. And remember not to talk to strangers."

After breakfast Louis took the train into Grand Central Station. As the skyscrapers of the city loomed into view through the grimy window, Louis felt a nervous twinge in his stomach. Getting to Yankee Stadium was easy—you just got off at 125th Street and rode the subway a few stops north. But Queens was on the other side of Manhattan. Louis had only been to Queens once, when he and his father had flown out of LaGuardia Airport to visit his grandparents in Chicago, and they had driven instead of taking the subway.

The train pulled into Grand Central Station a little past nine, and Louis was carried by a stampede of commuters up the stairs and onto the main concourse. He tucked himself behind a trash can while looking for the entrance to the subway. The sound in the concourse was similar to the sound right after a game ended at Yankee Stadium, a buzz like the vibrating of thousands of oversize bees. Except these bees wore noisy shoes and cleared their throats and sometimes shouted at one another.

Eventually the crowd broke, and Louis caught a glimpse of the sign for the subway. He briefly had to fight against the tide of commuters and was knocked sideways by the wake of a passing briefcase, but he finally made it to the ticket kiosk and paid his fifteen cents for a token. The subway car was only half full—maybe because most people were going in the opposite direction—and Louis found a spot on the bench. His mother had told him that the key to staying safe on the subway was to make sure that you never looked at anyone, so he stared out the window at the dark shapes in the passing tunnel. Every station a few more passengers would leak out of the train, and when they finally reached his stop in Forest Hills, only a few people remained.

Louis was briefly disoriented when he emerged from the subway station, but he showed the address to a newspaper vendor, and the man pointed him in the right direction. The streets near the station were lined with stores and restaurants, and Louis's hungry stomach was tempted by the smells of pizza and fresh donuts. The heavy accents around him were also different from the accents that Louis heard near Yankee Stadium, which seemed strange to him. How could people who lived on the same subway system sound so different?

The directions eventually led Louis to a brick apartment building on a quiet street lined with bushy trees. As he approached the building, two men were arguing on the steps. The first man, who was blocking the door, was short and bald with a thick mustache and sweat stains on his white collared shirt. The second man was wearing a dark suit and standing with his back to Louis.

"I can't let you in," the short man was saying. "Not without signed permission."

"Come on, buddy," the man in the suit said. His voice sounded vaguely familiar to Louis. "I don't want to have to drive out here again."

"Why do you need to go up there?"

"I showed you my card," the man in the suit said. "I'm from the Yankees. Our boys forgot to turn in some paperwork, and we're going to get all kinds of trouble from the commissioner if I don't get it. Pronto."

The short man stared at him, his fingers drumming on the edge of the door. The man in the suit jerked his thumb over his shoulder.

"You want a signed bat or something?" he asked. "I got one in my car."

The short man's eyes flickered down the block, and the man in the suit turned and pointed at a blue sedan. As his head swung toward the street, Louis realized why he had recognized the voice. It was Nathan Scully, the reporter from the locker room.

The short man glanced down at a business card in his hand and then begrudgingly stepped aside. "All right," he said. "Just be quick."

In the moment that followed a hundred thoughts flashed through Louis's head. His instinct was to retreat down the block, come back later for the package, and pretend that he hadn't seen Nathan. That would be the safest thing to do. But when Louis imagined the reporter rooting through the apartment, something turned in his stomach. Maybe he was only a kid, and maybe Nathan would do something bad to him, but nobody else was here to stand up for Mickey and Roger. Nobody else was here to stand up for the Yankees.

"Wait," Louis said. Two heads turned toward him, and Louis forced himself to climb the stairs of the building. "He doesn't work for the Yankees."

The short man slid back into the doorway, his arms folding across his chest. Nathan's eyes got narrow and mean.

"I've never seen this kid before in my life," Nathan said to the short man. "I told you why I'm here. And I gave you my card from the team."

"It's fake," Louis said. "He's a reporter. For the *Daily News.*"

"Oh, yeah?" the short man said.

Nathan laughed, but it wasn't a real laugh. "Come on. You must get crazy kids hanging around here all the time. Are you going to believe him or me?"

The short man glanced at Louis and then back at Nathan, and Louis could sense that he was wavering. For a moment Louis felt helpless, but then he remembered the keys. He reached into his pocket and pulled them out.

"Mr. Cerv gave me these," he said. "I'm supposed to mail a package for him."

The short man silently took the keys and stuck one into the lock. He twisted his wrist, and the bolt slid open and then closed. He looked at Louis for a long moment before turning to Nathan.

"You better get out of here," he said, his jaw bulging. "Are you trying to get me fired or something?"

Nathan smiled a slick smile. "Sorry for the misunderstanding."

"I'm not fooling," the short man said. His finger jutted toward Nathan. "I see you around here again and I'm calling the police."

Nathan slowly retreated down the steps, his hands up and the slick smile still on his face.

"Okay," he said. His eyes settled on Louis and the smile disappeared. "I'll see you around."

A moment later Nathan was striding down the block, the heels of his dress shoes clicking on the pavement. Louis waited until he had disappeared into the blue sedan before stepping into the building. When he was inside, the short man handed him the keys and gave him a friendly bob of the head.

"Thanks, kid," he said. "The apartment's on the third floor."

The stairwell smelled like wood polish and cat litter. Louis paused before unlocking the door—it felt weird to go into someone's apartment when they weren't there. As he stepped inside, however, his first feeling was disappointment. Louis didn't know exactly what he had expected, but this apartment looked just like a normal house. The furniture was bland, a few boring paintings hung on the walls, and the back windows had a view of a bunch of tennis courts. The only sign that this might be the home of professional baseball players was a chin-up bar in one of the doorways.

Bob Cerv had said that the package was on Roger's bed, so Louis wandered down the short hallway. Mickey was in the bedroom on the left, and Bob and Roger shared the bedroom on the right. Bob and Roger's room was as plain as the living room—just two twin beds, a nightstand, and a few dumbbells. It smelled strongly of aftershave. For some reason it seemed funny to Louis that Roger was married and had children but still had to share a bedroom with another man. It was like he was at camp or something.

The package was indeed on the bed. As Louis crossed the room he noticed two neat stacks of letters on the floor. He stood motionless for a moment, trying not to let his curiosity get the best of him, but the urge to take a quick peek was too strong. He leaned over and picked up a letter from the pile closer to his foot.

Dear Mr. Maris,

I'm eight years old and the Yankees are my favorite team. You are my favorite player. Please hit many more home runs. I hope you beat the Pirates in the World Series.

Sincerely,
Alex Kelly

Attached to the letter by a paper clip was a response in neat handwriting.

Dear Alex,

I am honored that I am your favorite player, and I will do my best to keep hitting home runs. Me and the guys sure want to beat the Pirates this year. We owe them from last fall.

Your friend,
Roger Maris

Louis smiled as he carefully replaced the letter, but his smile faded as he caught a glimpse of the top of the other pile. The words were scrawled in sloppy handwriting.

Hey hick,

This is the town of DiMaggio and Mick and the Babe and if you don't want to be here you can just go back to your cornfield. You think we can't find someone who can get one lousy hit in game seven? You can hit a hundred home runs and you'll still never be good enough to carry the Babe's jock.

I hope you break your leg, you bum.

Jerry Rollins

When Louis finished reading, his heart was racing, and his hands shook as he grabbed the package. He left the apartment as quickly as possible, making sure to lock the door behind him, and when he got to the front steps, he paused for a moment and took a deep breath of the fresh air. Louis wished that he'd never glanced at the letters. Was that entire second pile filled with more people like Jerry Rollins? And if it was, why was that pile so much bigger than the pile of fan mail? It wasn't fair. Roger played hard and had been the MVP of the league the previous year. Maybe he wasn't Mickey Mantle or Babe Ruth, but *nobody* was Mickey Mantle or Babe Ruth.

As Louis started back toward the subway station, he decided that he would never understand humans. The

Yankees were the best team in baseball, yet some of their fans were still writing the star right fielder and calling him names. In a weird way it made Louis feel better. If a whole stack of people were dumb enough to call Roger Maris a bum, then maybe Louis shouldn't mind so much when the kids in the neighborhood teased him. Maybe some people were just born mean.

CHAPTER EIGHT

Bottom of the Fourth

Louis was back in Grand Central Station the following Sunday morning, except this time he had permission to be there because his father had kept his promise and allowed Louis to go into the city and spend the night with his mother. They were supposed to meet under the departure board in the main concourse, but the moment he emerged from the tunnel she ambushed him with a huge hug.

"I'm so glad you're here," she said. "And I don't have to work at the restaurant tonight. We're going to have a great time."

They took the subway down to the East Village. Louis had brought a backpack that his stepmother had stuffed with extra socks, underwear, two T-shirts, and a toothbrush, and they dropped it off at his mother's apartment. The apartment was just one room, and it was so small that if you were lying in bed you could touch both the stove and the door of the bathroom with a broom handle. His mother had decorated the walls with black-and-white photographs and flyers for local concerts. Louis didn't recognize any of the names, but that didn't surprise him. He didn't know any of the singers who were popular at school either—whenever he listened to the radio it was a baseball game, not music.

After they dropped off his backpack, they walked over to Washington Square Park. His mother bought him a sandwich for lunch, and they sat on a bench with a view of the fountain while he ate. It was a warm Sunday afternoon, but the park was empty compared to Louis's last visit in the early spring. That time poets had been standing on the statues of famous people as they shouted lines of their work, and at least a dozen musicians had been gathered around the fountain, banging drums and playing saxophones and xylophones and guitars.

"What happened to all the musicians and poets?" Louis asked after he swallowed the final bite of his sandwich.

"There was a problem with the police in April," she said. "Maybe a week after you were here."

"What kind of problem?"

"Well, there's a new police commissioner, and he decided not to give a permit to the people who wanted to play music."

"Why?" Louis asked.

"Because he thought there were too many undesirable elements hanging around and ruining the park for decent people."

"What does that mean? 'Undesirable elements'?"

His mother was staring at the fountain. "Black people and beatniks."

"Are you a beatnik?" Louis asked.

She turned to him, an odd look on her face. "I don't know, Louis. I like folk music and modern poetry, but I don't want to label myself."

"Dad says that beatniks are ruining the country. He says that's why we didn't win in Korea."

"Your father has a lot of silly opinions." She patted his leg and then stood. "Let's go, kiddo. I've got a friend I want you to meet."

They walked a few blocks to a café. The walls inside were painted black, and people had scribbled lines of poetry and slogans on them with chalk. While his mother bought a coffee, Louis waited in the corner, trying to look inconspicuous. Nobody was dressed the way that people dressed in White Plains. The women had flat, natural hair like his mother, sometimes tucked into funny hats called berets, and the men were wearing sandals instead of real shoes. Maybe, Louis thought as he awkwardly pressed himself against the wall, this was the way his mother felt when she came out to the suburbs—like a cowboy among Indians.

His mother eventually returned with her coffee and led him to the back corner. The café was filled with people playing chess and another game that Louis didn't recognize. His mother stopped at a table where a man with a thick beard was reading a book and smoking a thin cigarette. Even though it was hot in the café, he was wearing a dark maroon sweater.

"Hi, Rod," his mother said.

The man looked up. He smiled when he saw Louis's mother, his teeth ivory outposts in a thicket of hair, and his brown eyes settled on Louis.

"So I finally get to meet your son," he said.

Louis's mother poked him in the shoulder. "Say hello, Louis."

"Hello," Louis said. "Mr. . . . ?"

As his voice trailed off, the man laughed.

"Call me Rod," he said. "We don't stand on formality here."

"Okay," Louis said. He paused. "Rod."

It felt funny to call an adult by a first name, and Louis almost expected his stepmother to appear from behind a table and give him a dirty look.

"Your mother says you're some kind of math whiz," Rod said after a moment.

Louis shrugged. "I don't know."

"She also says that you like baseball. Is that right?"

"Yeah."

"Say an outfielder gets six hits in twenty at bats. What's his average?"

".300," Louis said. "But that's easy. You just divide six by two."

"How about six hits in seventeen at bats?"

Louis squinted his eyes as he concentrated. "About .350. Maybe a little higher."

"I'd say you're pretty good at math," Rod said with a long look at Louis's mother. "You want to learn a new game?"

"Sure," Louis said.

As Louis soon discovered, the strange game that the other people in the café had been playing was backgammon. One team was black and the other team was white, and you moved your pieces around a board by rolling the dice. Rod was a good teacher, and Louis got the hang of it pretty quickly. He almost won the fourth game, and Rod leaned away from the board and glanced at his mother.

"We've got a natural," he said. "Just tell him to stay away from the gamblers in Times Square."

Louis gave the board a skeptical look. "People bet on backgammon?"

"People will bet on anything," his mother said.

"That's right," Rod said. "And here's a hint. If someone teaches you a game and half an hour later they want to bet money, you're about to be a sucker."

"So I shouldn't bet with you," Louis said.

Rob laughed. "No. I guess you shouldn't." He looked at Louis's mother. "Are you taking him to Folk City tonight?"

"The Gaslight," she said. "It's more . . . kid-friendly."

"What does that mean?" Louis asked.

"They don't serve booze," Rod said. He extended a palm. "Good to meet you, Louis."

"Good to meet you," Louis said as they shook hands.

As they left the café and headed down Sixth Avenue, Louis wondered why his mother had introduced him to Rod. Was he just a friend—or something more? In the early summer his mother had taken him to an art museum with a tall poet named Chad, and she and Chad had held hands as they strolled through the galleries. But Louis hadn't heard Chad's name since. Had Rod replaced Chad?

"What's the Gaslight?" he asked after they had gone a couple of blocks.

"A music club. You'll love it."

"Will there be other kids there?"

"No." They walked another dozen feet in silence. "Listen, Louis. I don't get to see you much, so it's important to me that I get to show you some of the things that I love. It's like the way you used to ask me to listen to baseball on the radio. Do you know what I mean?"

"I wish you'd come to a game," Louis said.

She stopped and bent over so that her face was even with his. "I will come to a game," she said, her brown eyes unblinking. "I promise."

When they got back to the apartment, his mother took a shower while Louis read the sports page. The Yankees were in Baltimore and had beaten the Orioles the previous night 2-1. Mantle had hit his thirty-second home run—putting him three behind Maris—and both men were still on pace to break Babe Ruth's record.

When his mother got out of the shower, she made dinner on her tiny stove. She wasn't much of a cook, so she just opened a can of beans, cut up some hot dogs, and boiled the mixture until everything was hot. After they finished eating, they walked back toward Washington Square Park. The Gaslight was on a busy street lined with clothing stores and Italian restaurants. A set of uneven stone steps led down from the sidewalk to a pair of swinging wooden doors, and his mother smiled at him as she stepped inside.

"Here we go," she said.

Louis's first feeling as he passed through the doors was that he had entered a cave. The room was crowded with people, and the ceiling was so low that the taller men had to duck their heads. The air was moist with the sweat and steam of bodies. On the far side of the room two men were playing on a tiny stage, lit by a few fixed spotlights. A metal bucket sat beside the performers, and as Louis squinted his eyes, he noticed a steady trickle of water running from a leak in the ceiling into the bucket.

"Over here," his mother said.

She had chosen a table near the back, and Louis gratefully settled into his seat. The music coming from the stage was different from anything he had heard at school or in his father's house—the voices were raspy, and the guitars had a strange rhythm and twang. His mother leaned forward and whispered in his ear.

"The singer is Ramblin' Jack Elliot," she said. "The kid behind him with the guitar and harmonica is only eight years older than you."

Louis took a closer look at the stage. The younger singer was smooth-faced with narrow eyebrows and a sharp nose. A worn cowskin jacket was draped over his skinny shoulders.

"Who is he?" Louis asked.

"His mother named him Robert Zimmerman, but he goes by Bob Dylan. Like the poet. He's going to be real big someday."

Louis nodded and settled back into his chair. He wondered what it would be like to change your name. Would you feel different? Would you act different? It was kind of a funny question when you thought about it . . . would Mickey Mantle hit as many home runs if his name were Louis May?

When the song finished, Louis waited for applause, but instead the people in the audience started snapping their fingers. He glanced at his mother, curious.

"Why don't they clap?" he asked.

His mother pointed at a window near the stage. "That's an air shaft," she said. "The sound goes right up to the neighbors and the neighbors call the police."

"The neighbors don't mind the music?"

She smiled. "Sometimes they do. Sometimes they don't."

The next song started, and his mother's attention returned to the stage. The music was good, but Louis's focus began to drift, and he started daydreaming about the Yankees. In his imagination he picked the perfect bat for Mickey to hit a game-winning home run, and Louis could picture himself standing in front of the clubhouse, head modestly down-cast, as Mr. Houk thanked him for saving the season. He imagined Mickey patting him on the back and Roger giving him a wink and—

"Wake up," a voice said in his ear.

Louis opened his eyes. His mother was smiling at him, her hand on his arm.

"Time for you to turn into a pumpkin," she said.

The street outside the club was packed with people, and they picked their way through the crowd to Sixth Avenue. It was still hot outside, and as Louis lay next to his mother in the unfamiliar bed, he worried that he might not be able to fall asleep. But he focused on the steady sound of her breathing and the cozy feeling of being tucked in the tiny apartment, and before too long he was dreaming again.

Louis awoke to the sounds of rush hour blaring through the open window—honking and shouting and the occasional squeal of brakes. His mother was frying eggs on the tiny stove. She put them on top of a slice of Spam, and they ate with Louis sitting at the little table and his mother perched on the edge of the bed. Louis didn't have to be on a train until after lunch, so they spent a lazy few hours wandering around the local stores. His mother bought him a used copy of a book about Cy Young, which was nice of her because she'd never even heard of Cy Young.

They had an early lunch at a deli near Grand Central Station. A radio was playing the news in the background, and Louis was halfway through his meatloaf when he heard the announcer mention the Yankees. He cocked his ear.

"Commissioner Ford Frick ruled today that any player who breaks Babe Ruth's home run record must do it in the first 154 games of the season, not the full 162 games on the schedule. That means that if Roger Maris or Mickey Mantle hit their sixty-first home run in the one hundred fifty-fifth game of the season, their name will have an asterisk in the record book."

"That's not fair," Louis said.

He suddenly realized that his voice had been loud, and he flushed as the man behind the counter and his mother stared at him.

"What's not fair?" his mother asked.

"Commissioner Frick was friends with Babe Ruth," Louis said. "He even wrote a book for him. Back when he was a reporter."

"It doesn't matter," the man behind the counter said. "Nobody's catching the Babe. Maris had thirty last July, and he finished with thirty-nine."

Louis kept his mouth shut. Roger had hurt his ribs in August of the previous season, which was why he had struggled at the plate. But maybe that was the man's point.

Anything could happen in a baseball season. You could hurt your ribs or go in a slump or have other teams start to pitch around you—

"Finish your lunch," his mother said, interrupting his thoughts. "Your father will kill me if you miss your train."

Louis scarfed down the rest of his meatloaf, and ten minutes later they were back in the main concourse of Grand Central Station. His mother gave him a long hug, and Louis felt something wet against the side of his face.

"I wish you were coming back with me to White Plains," he said when they separated.

"I know, baby," she said. "But that's not me. And the only thing I've learned in this life is that you have to try to be yourself."

She gave him a last pat on the cheek, and Louis turned and walked toward the entrance to his platform. As he started down the stairs he glanced back over his shoulder. The previous night in the café and music hall his mother had seemed at home, but here, with businessmen in suits and elegantly dressed women swirling around her, she once again looked like a puzzle piece that didn't quite fit. She was dabbing at her eyes with the sleeve of her dark sweater, but when she noticed him looking back at her, she smiled and waved good-bye.

CHAPTER NINE

Top of the Fifth

It seemed to Louis as if the Yankees' road trip lasted for a month, but it was actually only fourteen games. They went from Chicago to Baltimore to Washington to Boston before finally returning home on July 25 for a doubleheader against the White Sox. While the team was out of town, Louis listened to the games on the radio and studied the box scores. Roger hit three home runs on the road trip, but Mickey smacked an amazing eight and now had 37 for the season—one more than Roger. Both men were still on pace to break Babe Ruth's record, and every day it seemed as if there were more and more stories in the paper about their chase.

Louis arrived at Yankee Stadium the morning of the doubleheader to unpack the buses. The players started to straggle into the clubhouse in the mid-afternoon, eyes bleary. Roger, Mickey, and Bob arrived together, and Mickey rubbed Louis's head.

"I hope you missed us," he said.

Bob waited for Mickey and Roger to go to their lockers and then leaned down to Louis.

"Thanks for taking care of that thing," he said quietly.

"Sure." Louis lowered his own voice to just above a whisper. "A reporter was trying to get into your apartment."

Bob squatted down and put his hand on Louis's shoulder. "Oh, yeah? Which one?"

"Nathan Scully. From the *Daily News*."

Bob's eyes narrowed. "He's a snake." He paused. "But don't you worry about it, okay? This is adult stuff. Me and the guys will keep our eyes open."

"Okay," Louis said.

The first game started at six. In the fourth inning, with Bobby Richardson on second base, Roger hammered his thirty-seventh home run to right field. Mickey, the next batter, strode to the plate, and two pitches later he slammed his own home run to left field. But Roger wasn't done, and in the bottom of the eighth he hit another home run to right field. This time Mickey couldn't respond—he popped to the catcher—and they ended the game tied with 38 home runs. The Yankees won 5-2, and in the clubhouse between the games Mickey shouted to Roger, "Hey, how many do you plan on hitting in the second game?"

Roger, who was carefully oiling his favorite glove by his locker, glanced up. "Depends how many good pitches I see," he said. "How about you?"

"I'm just getting warmed up," Mickey said with a grin.

But it turned out that Roger was the one who was just getting warmed up. He bashed a home run in the fourth inning and another in the sixth to help lead the Yankees to a 12-0 rout, while Mickey went hitless. The game ended with the

Yankees now leading Detroit by half a game for the pennant, and even though the players were clearly exhausted from the doubleheader and the long road trip, they were laughing and joking in the clubhouse after the game.

Louis tried to ignore the celebration and finish his work as quickly as possible. It was already eleven thirty, and he knew that if he missed the last train his stepmother would murder him—she was already unhappy that he was going to get home after midnight. He therefore wasn't paying much attention as he cut through the crowd of reporters around Roger's locker, but as he got on his hands and knees to pull out the pair of dirty cleats, he heard an odd tone in Roger's voice. It sounded as if he was annoyed.

". . . I can't control that," he said as Louis focused. "I just go out there and play ball."

Louis slowly stood. He was just behind Roger, and eight or nine reporters with notebooks were crowding them on all sides. Louis didn't understand why they had to stand so close.

"Did you notice that people seemed to be cheering louder for Mickey than for you?" one of the reporters asked. He had a round face and a thick pair of glasses.

Roger shrugged. "Well, Mickey's been a Yankee for a long time."

"Does it bother you?" a familiar voice asked. It was Nathan Scully. He was standing just a few feet from Louis, his pencil poised like a knife.

"Nope," Roger said. "I'm glad the fans appreciate Mickey."

"It would bother me," Nathan said. "To know that most fans are pulling for one of my teammates."

"Well, I'm not you," Roger said. The annoyed edge that Louis had first noticed had returned to his voice. "Maybe that's why I don't go snooping around other people's apartments."

Nathan somehow managed to look innocent. "What's that supposed to mean?"

"It means no more questions," Roger said.

As Roger pushed his way through the crowd of reporters, a few of them started to grumble, and when he disappeared into the trainer's room, the grumbles turned into muttered insults. One of the reporters turned to Mickey, who had just finished answering questions at his own locker.

"I don't know why he has to be so sour all the time," the reporter said.

"He's still got a bum hamstring," Mickey said. "Let him get his treatment."

"You tell him that he needs to talk to us," Nathan said.

Mickey shook his head. "He answered a bunch of your questions. And why do you fellows always need to talk to me and Rog, huh? Go talk to Bill. He pitched a heck of a game tonight."

"Come on, Mick," another reporter said. "Everyone wants to hear about you guys. And we've got stories to write."

Mickey pulled a piece of paper out of his locker, scribbled a few words on it, and then waved to Louis.

"Take this to Rog," he said when Louis reached his side. "And grab him a beer, okay?"

Louis got a can of beer from the clubhouse man and then went into the trainer's room. The room always smelled like a Ben-Gay factory, and the ice machine in the corner constantly whined. Roger was sitting on one of the trainer's padded tables, meticulously wrapping and unwrapping an Ace bandage around his wrist. The room was otherwise deserted.

"Hey, kid," he said.

Louis silently handed him the beer and the note. Roger popped open the beer and took a long swig before glancing at Mickey's messy handwriting. He snorted when he saw what was on the paper.

"Mickey says that I should get back out there and take my beating like a man," he said. "What do you think?"

"I think they're a bunch of jerks."

Roger smiled. "Ah, they're just trying to do their jobs. Most of them, anyway. But I get tired of answering the same questions over and over again."

"Why were they asking you about the crowd?" Louis asked.

"Probably to stir up trouble. And because they know it sells papers. The truth is that this town has already made up its mind about me—the fans and the reporters and everyone. I'm not a real Yankee."

"My dad says they didn't like Mickey Mantle at first."

Roger raised an eyebrow. "Is that right?"

"They said he was a rube and a hick and would never be as good as Joe DiMaggio. Some people cheered when he tripped on the drain in the 1951 World Series and tore up his knee."

Roger shook his head. "People can be awful hard to please. But I can't complain. If my friends at home heard me whining about being a baseball player, they'd probably punch me in the nose. Facing a pack of reporters is a heck of a lot easier than going down into a mine or working for the railroad."

"You're from North Dakota," Louis said. He'd read that on Roger's baseball card.

"A city called Fargo." Roger paused, a distant look in his eye. "It's different out there. Life can be real hard, so people stick together. When my brother got polio, I don't think a day went by that a neighbor didn't bring over food or slip a little money in the mailbox to help with the doctor's bills."

"Your brother had polio?"

"Yup. He was a great athlete before he got sick."

"My stepbrother's a good athlete," Louis said.

"Is he older or younger?"

"Older."

"Maybe you'll catch up. That's what happened to me."

Louis shook his head. "I don't think so."

"What happened to your dad?" Roger asked.

"I live with my dad and my stepmother. My mother's in New York."

"Your folks are divorced?"

"Yeah."

"How long?"

"A year."

They were quiet for a minute or two. Louis stared at one of the posters on the wall: a medical diagram of a shoulder joint. He knew that he should go finish his work so that he would make the last train to White Plains, but he didn't want to let this moment end.

"What did your parents say about the divorce?" Roger finally asked.

"They said that it wasn't my fault. That my mom just wanted to live in the city and my dad wanted to live in the suburbs. But I'm not a little kid. I know that my mom doesn't want to be like the other moms."

"How much do you see her?"

"Once or twice a month."

"I bet she misses you like crazy," Roger said. "There's not a single hour of the day when I don't think of my kids back in Kansas City. I only get to call them once a week because the long distance costs so much."

They were quiet again, and for a horrible moment Louis thought that tears were going to start leaking out of the corners of his eyes. They always seemed to come when he talked about his mother. But Louis wasn't going to let himself cry in front of Roger Maris, so he bit the edge of his tongue as hard as he could, and the pain soon replaced everything else.

"Well, there's no sense in us moping about it," Roger finally said. "It's okay to miss people. It just means you care about them, right?"

"Sure," Louis said.

Roger pushed himself to his feet, the beer and the Ace bandage forgotten on the table.

"Time for me to face the music," he said. "Although I sure wish there were some way for me to get out of this locker room without walking past those reporters."

Louis glanced around the room, his mind racing. His eyes eventually settled on the large towel bin in the corner. One of his assignments was to wheel the bin down the hall to the laundry room. He glanced from the bin to Roger and back, and Roger gave him an amused look.

"You got some sort of plan?" he asked.

"Maybe you could hide in the towel bin," Louis said.

"And I could push you past the reporters to the laundry room."

Roger gave the bin a skeptical look. "You think I'd fit in there?"

"Maybe."

Roger stared at the bin for another few seconds, and then a slow smile spread across his face. "It would be a pretty good trick, wouldn't it?"

"Yeah," Louis said. "And since the reporters think you're still in here, they'll probably stand around waiting."

"Well, I owe them one." Roger gave the bin one last look. "What the heck? Let's give it a shot."

They dumped the towels out on the floor, and then Roger squeezed into the bin. His knees were wedged against his chin, and his thick arms were jammed against the canvas sides. Louis carefully tucked towels around Roger's body until only his head was sticking out above a sea of white cotton.

"I bet you never saw a grown man hiding in a towel bin before," Roger said with a sheepish smile.

Louis mirrored his smile and then tossed the last few towels over Roger's close-cropped hair. He had to lean hard against the bin to make it move, and once it was going it was as hard to turn as a battleship. When he staggered into the main locker room, the reporters parted to let him pass. All except for Nathan Scully.

"Hey, kid," Nathan said as the bin ground to a halt. His hand touched the edge of the canvas, just a foot from Roger's head.

"I've got to get these to the laundry room," Louis said.

Nathan gave him a sour look. "Is that big ape coming out anytime soon?"

"Any second now," Louis said.

Louis thought he heard a faint snicker from the cart, but Nathan didn't seem to notice because he just grunted and stepped aside. Louis wheeled the cart through the room, collecting dirty towels from the floor, until he came to Roger's locker. He took a quick peek back at the reporters. They were all preoccupied with their notebooks or conversations, and Louis grabbed Roger's shoes and wallet and quickly wrapped them in a towel.

A minute later he was heading down the hall, and when Louis finally closed the laundry room door, his heart was pounding—either from his nerves or the weight of the bin. He pulled the towels off Roger's head.

"Here we are," he said.

Roger slowly straightened, more towels falling from his body. "I thought I was going to pass out," he said. "That thing smelled like the Devil's armpit."

Louis pointed at the wallet and shoes. "I grabbed those for you."

Roger glanced at them and then shook his head, a faint smile on his face. "Pretty clever," he said. "You should work for the CIA or something."

Roger put on his shoes and shoved the wallet in his pocket. He was wearing just a pair of pants and an undershirt, but it was a warm night. As Louis started to load the dirty towels back into the bin, Roger patted him on the back.

"Thanks, Lucky," he said.

He turned and his hand was on the door when Louis spoke, his heart pounding even harder than when he had been pushing the cart.

"Why do you do it, Mr. Maris? If you don't like reporters

and miss your family and everything else? It can't just be about money, can it?"

Roger slowly turned around and stared at Louis, an odd expression on his face. "Why do you get on a train and come to this stadium to pick up dirty towels and scrub muddy shoes and not make a dime?"

"Because it's baseball," Louis said.

"That's right," Roger said. "It's baseball. And when I'm standing in that batter's box and the pitcher starts his windup, there are no reporters or fans. No bad articles or boos or anything else. There's just a ball. And when you hit it right, there's no better feeling in the world."

CHAPTER TEN

Bottom of the Fifth

That doubleheader seemed to mark a turning point in the race for Ruth's record. Players in previous years occasionally had made early runs at the record only to fade away, but something about that barrage of home runs in late July convinced the baseball world that this season it was actually possible that someone might finally pass the Babe. With that realization even more hordes of reporters descended upon the clubhouse, and articles began to appear in non-sport magazines such as *Time* and *Newsweek*. Scientists were conducting tests to see whether the ball was more lively than it had been in 1927, and the papers were filled with arguments over whether the pitchers of today were better or worse than the pitchers Ruth had faced.

Louis overheard conversations about Mickey and Roger on the train and at the pizza parlor and in the line at the grocery store. And every time he had the same reaction—he wanted to leap forward and say that he, Louis May, had one of the best seats in Yankee Stadium for the greatest home run race of all time. But he always stifled the urge and kept that remarkable fact to himself.

Roger didn't pull any more tricks to hide from the reporters, but the damage was already done. It was obvious to Louis when he read the paper that everyone was rooting for Mickey. And Louis had to admit that he knew why. Mickey teased the reporters, told them jokes, and always gave them an interesting quote or two. Roger, on the other hand, would stand in front of his locker, arms crossed, and answer the questions as if he were being staked to an anthill.

As July turned into August, the race remained neck and neck, and when the Yankees left for a short road trip, Maris had 42 home runs and Mantle had 44. The night before the team departed, Louis again helped pack the vans, and the next morning he awoke long after breakfast. As Louis stretched in bed he realized that it had been at least a week since he had flipped through his baseball card collection. Today would be a perfect lazy day to do some organizing. He reached under the bed, his hand fumbling for the cardboard boxes.

But they weren't there.

Louis leaped onto the floor, his hand reaching farther back. Still nothing. A pit formed in his stomach, and Louis flipped up the bed's dust ruffle. There was a tennis ball and a library book and few bits of lint, but no boxes. His cards were gone.

A moment later Louis was dashing down the stairs, his brain frantically sorting through the possibilities. Had his stepmother, in the midst of one of her cleaning fits, accidentally thrown them out? Had somebody robbed the house? But if a person was going to rob a house, why would they leave the jewelry and television and only take his baseball cards?

Louis skidded to a stop in the kitchen, his socks slipping on the polished linoleum. His stepmother was sitting at the table, coffee in one hand and one of her *Better Homes and Gardens* books in the other. She glanced up at him.

"What have I told you about running in the house?" she asked.

"My card collection is missing." His breath was coming in quick pants. "Two boxes. Have you seen them?"

"Your cards?"

"Baseball cards," Louis said. "In boxes."

His stepmother's eyes returned to her book. "Have you checked under your bed?"

"Of course I checked under my bed," Louis said, trying to keep his tone from being snippy. His stepmother got upset when his tone was snippy. "Maybe someone stole them."

"Honestly, Louis. Who would steal a bunch of pieces of paper?"

"Money is just pieces of paper. And lots of people want to steal that." She kept reading. "Maybe it was Bryce."

His stepmother arched an eyebrow. "I'm sure that Bryce wouldn't touch your cards. But he's playing in the back-yard if you want to ask him."

Louis dashed upstairs to get dressed and then sprinted down to the backyard. Bryce was standing next to the garage, tossing a baseball onto the roof and catching it when it rolled off.

"Did you take my baseball cards?" Louis asked.

"What?"

"My baseball cards are gone."

"Why would I want your baseball cards? I don't even like baseball cards."

Bryce tossed the ball again, his eyes locked on the roof. Louis turned away, frustrated. Talking to Bryce was worse than talking to the television—at least the television occasionally would say something interesting. Louis had taken a few steps toward the house when Bryce spoke behind him.

"Maybe I know who took them."

Louis spun around. "Who?"

"I'll make you a deal," Bryce said, tucking his glove under his arm. "You help me fix up the stickball field, and I'll tell you what happened."

"I thought that Alex and Doug were going to help you with the field."

Bryce shrugged. "They're lazy. We got a deal or not?"

"Sure," Louis said.

Bryce spat on his hand and stuck it out. Louis did the same thing, and they shook. Bryce sealed everything with spit. As they walked down to the field, Louis tried to keep from getting angry. It wasn't fair of Bryce to refuse to tell him about the baseball cards without Louis paying tribute, but that was just Bryce. And there was no point in arguing because once Bryce made up his mind, that was it.

"What do you want to do?" Louis asked when they were standing by the enormous chimney.

"I want it to look like a real field," Bryce said.

Louis's eyes swept over the vacant lot. The grass was trampled around the base paths, and a log was dug into the ground to serve as a pitching rubber, but otherwise it looked nothing like a baseball diamond.

"How do you want to do that?" Louis asked.

Bryce kicked a pebble. "I thought you might have some ideas. You know, since you're spending so much time at Yankee Stadium."

Louis tried to keep from looking surprised. Not only did Bryce rarely mention Louis's job as a batboy, he had never, *ever*, asked for Louis's advice. On any subject. Louis turned his attention back to the field, this time with real interest.

"We need foul lines," he said. "Real bases. We should mow the infield. Set up a rope fence in the outfield for home runs. And the pitching rubber should be sunk deeper into the ground so people don't trip on it."

Bryce looked doubtfully at the field. "How are we going to get foul lines? Or bases?"

"We'll make them," Louis said.

And that's exactly what they did. Bryce convinced his mother to take four old seed bags from the garage, fill them with rice, and sew them shut. Louis found a long spool of string, ran it down the foul line to serve as a marker, and then drew the line with flour. Bryce mowed the infield while Louis dug the rubber into the ground, and they collaborated on constructing the outfield fence out of wooden stakes and a spool of twine.

Louis worked as hard as he could, but the entire time he couldn't help thinking about his baseball cards. He had been collecting for five years now, and Louis felt as if he could remember how he had gotten every single player. His first pack had been stuffed in his Christmas stocking, and it had contained a Sandy Koufax rookie card, which was still one of Louis's ten favorite cards. How many nickel packs had he bought since then? A few hundred? A thousand?

He had spent almost every penny of his allowance on the packs for at least five years.

And then there were the cards that Louis had acquired in years of careful trading. He had swapped a 1958 Tony Kubek card with a rabid Yankees fan for the Ted Williams card from 1953, the season the Splendid Splinter had just 91 at bats because he'd begun the year flying fighter planes for the Marines in Korea. He had traded a 1958 Hoyt Wilhelm card to a Baltimore fan for a 1957 Warren Spahn, which was the year Warren had finally won the Cy Young. And he had miraculously traded an assortment of mediocre Dodgers for a 1955 Willie Mays card, which featured a black-and-white photo of Willie staring intently toward a pitcher, the muscles of his forearms bulging as he squeezed his bat.

Now they were all gone. . . . Koufax and Mays and Williams and Spahn and hundreds and hundreds more. And not only were the cards gone, but so was all of the information that they contained. Batting averages and home run totals and personal details and facts. When Louis was listening to a game on the radio he loved to be able to line up the cards for the opposing teams. It was almost like being at the ballpark—you could see the player's face and imagine him at the plate or in the field.

"Hey," Bryce said, breaking Louis's train of thought. "Any other ideas?"

Louis took a long moment to examine their work. The outfield was still overgrown and the pitcher's mound wasn't a mound and the bases looked a little droopy, but it was definitely a field. No longer would there be arguments over whether a ball was a foul or a home run—now there were lines and a simple rope fence. The pitcher would never again trip over the rubber. And balls in the infield would bounce almost normally instead of having to fight their way through weeds and tall grass.

"We're done," Louis said. "Where are my cards?"

"What cards?"

"Come on. A deal's a deal."

"Fine," Bryce said, his eyes avoiding Louis. "I traded your cards to Ivan for a bike."

Bryce turned and walked back toward the house, leaving Louis standing alone in the field with his mouth hanging open. Ivan was a year older than Bryce, and he was the neighborhood bully. He stole lunch money, pushed kids into puddles on rainy days, and generally terrorized everyone smaller than him. Even Bryce wasn't immune. A month earlier Bryce had been playing football with some friends, and Ivan had walked out of his house, grabbed the ball from Bryce, and kept it.

And now Ivan had the cards. Louis felt a surge of anger and frustration. Why would Bryce steal his collection? And what was Louis supposed to do now? If he went to his stepmother, she'd just take Bryce's side—and Bryce would probably lie anyway.

Louis knew that he only had one real option, so he went to the front porch and waited on the stairs. His father returned home from work about an hour later, and as he walked up the driveway, Louis stood to meet him.

"Hey, champ," his father said. He must have noticed something in Louis's expression because he paused on the porch. "What's wrong?"

"Bryce stole my baseball cards," Louis said.

His father glanced at him and then wearily settled into the wicker chair. "Are you sure?"

"He admitted it. And he already traded them with another kid."

A long moment passed. And then his father pulled out his wallet. "How much would it cost to replace them?"

"You can't replace them," Louis said. "Not all of them."

"Why not?"

"Because I've been working on this collection for five years."

Louis's voice had risen, and he tried to take a breath to calm himself. He knew that it wouldn't help if he raised his voice.

"Listen," his father said after another pause. "I can go in the house and tell Bryce to return the cards. But I think you're at an age when you need to start handling these problems for yourself."

"Bryce is bigger than me. And older."

"Of course he is. But standing up for yourself has nothing to do with size, Louis. He's picking on you because he doesn't think you'll do anything about it."

Louis spoke without thinking. "He's picking on me because he knows you won't say anything to him in front of my stepmother."

The words hung in the air for one frozen moment, and then his father's face turned red. "That's enough," he said. "Go to your room."

Louis turned on his heel and stalked upstairs. It was totally unfair—Bryce stole Louis's prized card collection, and yet Louis was the one who got in trouble. His father could get as mad as he wanted, but Louis knew that he was right. Bryce never got punished for anything because his stepmother thought that Bryce was perfect, and his father was too much of a chicken to argue with her. And Louis's mother, who might have actually stood up for him, hadn't even bothered to call since Louis visited her apartment in New York.

As Louis lay on his bed listening to the sounds of dinner downstairs, tears of frustration burning in his eyes, one thing was clear. If he wanted to get his cards back, he was going to have to do it himself.

CHAPTER ELEVEN

Top of the Sixth

The Yankees returned home on August 14 with a three-and-a-half game lead on the Tigers for the pennant. The home run race was still front-page news almost every day, and when Louis got his late summer haircut the barber asked, "You want Maris or Mantle?" Louis blurted "Maris," and the barber gave him a short crew cut that made the hair on the back of his head look like a geyser.

Even though Louis was still distraught about his cards, he was glad that the team was back in town—and he practically skipped to the ballpark to unload the gear. Since Louis wasn't strong enough to help with the heaviest trunks, Gabe told him to unpack the players' lockers. Louis started with the cleats. One of the last pairs belonged to Mickey, and as Louis carried them across the room, he felt something bumping around inside the toe of the shoe. He tentatively reached inside, his fingers fumbling against leather, and withdrew a thin wallet. When he flipped it open, Mickey's face stared up at him from a driver's license.

"Great," Gabe said when Louis showed him the wallet. "Mick called this morning and said that he was missing it. We'll put it in the manager's office, and he can pick it up tomorrow."

"But what if he needs it tonight?"

Gabe shrugged. "Maybe he can come and get it."

"I can deliver it to him," Louis said.

"Do you know where he lives?"

"Yeah. In Queens."

Gabe gave him a long look. "Aren't you kind of young to be taking the subway all the way to Queens?"

"I did it before," Louis said.

Gabe stared down at the wallet before finally flicking his head at the lockers. "Finish those cleats and then go."

Half an hour later Louis was back on the subway. This time it was less nerve-racking because he knew where he was going, but he still avoided making eye contact with anyone. When he finally reached the apartment building, he was going to ring the bell, but a woman came out the front door just as he reached the top of the steps and let him inside. Louis went upstairs and knocked, and a moment later Bob Cerv opened the door.

"Hey, Lucky," he said. "What are you doing here?"

Louis held out the wallet. "Mr. Mantle left this in his cleats."

Bob shook his head, a bemused smile on his face. "We

should staple that thing to his hip." He opened the door a little wider. "Come in, kid."

Mickey was dealing cards to Roger at the kitchen table, and in the background a record was playing a song that Louis actually recognized: "I Fall to Pieces" by Patsy Cline, which had been everywhere for the last few weeks and was his stepmother's new favorite.

"Lucky just saved your night," Bob said as he tossed the wallet on the table. "Unless you plan on making your date pay for dinner."

Mickey glanced at the wallet and then up at Louis.

"You came all the way out here with my wallet?" he asked.

"Yes, sir."

"Well, that's awful decent of you."

Mickey reached into the wallet and pulled out a few bills. As he held them out, Louis shook his head.

"I was just doing my job, Mr. Mantle."

"Come on, kid," Mickey said. "At least take a buck. Get yourself some ice cream or something on the way home."

Louis glanced at the money and reluctantly took a dollar. He turned and was halfway to the door when Mickey spoke behind him.

"Are you too good to spend an afternoon in Queens?" he asked.

Louis turned around, confused.

"If you're going to come all the way out here, you may as well stay awhile," Roger said. "Play some cards. Have a pop."

Louis slowly walked back to the kitchen table and sat

down. He was obviously excited that Mickey and Roger had asked him to stay, but he was also nervous—what exactly was he supposed to do? The only card game he ever played was Go Fish, and he was pretty sure that baseball stars didn't play kids' games.

"Are you Italian?" Mickey asked when Louis was settled.

"I don't think so," Louis said.

"You look Italian. And we call you Lucky, so you could be a mobster. Like Lucky Luciano."

Louis knew that Mickey was teasing, but he wasn't sure how to respond. "My last name is May," he finally said.

Mickey grinned. "Good, so you're one of the M&M Boys. I guess it's a trio now . . . Maris, Mantle, and May."

Bob rolled his eyes. "Maris, Mantle, and May sounds like a moving company."

"Then we'll change our nickname," Mickey said. "Alert the press. Instead of the M&M Boys we will now be known as 3M."

"I think I have to hit some home runs first," Louis said.

The men laughed, and Louis's back relaxed a little bit against his chair.

"So what do you do when we're out of town?" Mickey asked. "Do you have school or something?"

"It's August," Roger said. "Of course he doesn't have school."

"It starts in a couple of weeks," Louis said.

"What about girls? Do you have a girlfriend?"

Louis tried to keep his nose from wrinkling. "A girlfriend?"

"He's too young for girls," Roger said.

"What does that mean?" Mickey asked. "I was never too young for girls."

Roger smiled, a glint in his eye. "We know, Mick."

Roger and Mickey and Bob all laughed, and Louis joined them, even though he wasn't sure what was so funny. When they had all caught their breath, Mickey again focused on Louis.

"Really," he said. "What do you do? Get in fights? Light things on fire?"

"Last week I helped my stepbrother fix his stickball field."

"You play stickball?" Mickey asked.

Louis shook his head. "Not much."

"Why not?"

"I'm pretty bad."

"What does that have to do with anything?" Mickey asked. "It's just for fun, right?"

Louis tried to keep from laughing—this time for real. "No offense, Mr. Mantle, but when you were growing up, I bet you weren't the last one picked to play."

"I guess I wasn't," Mickey said with a strange smile.

"Why are you the last one picked?" Roger asked. "You've got a good arm."

"I can't hit," Louis said. "And I get nervous when I try to make a catch."

"We all get nervous," Bob said. "There are days when that ball goes up in the air, and I just start whispering Hail Marys."

Roger stood, walked over to the sink, and rummaged in a cabinet. He pulled out a plunger and tugged on the wood shaft. It separated from the rubber with a pop.

"Let's see your swing," he said, handing the wood shaft to Louis.

"Here?" Louis asked with a nervous glance at the furniture.

"Yeah, here."

Louis slowly stepped away from the table. He could feel the eyes of the three players on him as he took a tentative swing.

"No," Mickey said. "Let it rip. Like you're trying to hit a home run."

Louis swung again, this time with more force.

"We need a ball," Mickey said.

He opened a drawer next to the table, pulled out a roll of masking tape, and spun the tape around his finger until he had a thick clump. He tossed it underhand toward Louis, and Louis tried to keep his eyes on it as he swung as hard as possible. He missed badly, and the ball landed on the floor behind him.

"That's okay," Roger said. "But your head's moving too much."

"Tell him why that matters," Bob said.

"Listen," Roger said. "Imagine that you're holding a gun and you're trying to shoot a target." Louis closed his eyes and tried to picture it in his head. "Pretend that you're standing on an outdoor elevator. The first time you take a shot, the elevator doesn't move. But the second time it drops a floor just before you pull the trigger. Do you think you have a better chance of hitting the target the first time or the second time?"

"You're confusing the kid," Mickey said. "In fact, you're

confusing me. And they pay me to play this game."

"It's easier to hit if I can keep my eyes on the same level," Louis said.

"Exactly," Roger said. "It gives your brain one less thing to worry about. So don't lunge. Stay in a crouch and take a small step forward, not down."

Louis tried another swing. Mickey stepped forward, looking frustrated.

"We're making this too complicated," he said. "Hitting's real easy. Just keep your balance and try to put on a good swing."

Bob snorted. "That works for you because you've got more talent in your big toe than the rest of us have in our whole bodies." He stood and twirled on his toes like a model. "Take a good look at me, kid. Do I look like a professional ball player? Or do I look like a guy you might see walking down the street?"

Mickey reached over and patted Bob's stomach. "They're not putting you on any pinup posters, big guy."

"That's right," Bob said. He waved a hand at Mickey and Roger. "I'm not a natural like these two. I'm not really fast or really strong, but I've still gotten a chance to play pro ball. You know why?"

"Why?"

"Because I don't get in my own way." Bob's forefinger tapped his temple. "Baseball is played up here, kid. A lot of guys strike out before they even walk out of the dugout. You've got to pick up that bat and believe that something good is going to happen. And if you strike out, you've got to forget about it the second the ball hits the catcher's glove. Because there's always tomorrow."

Bob picked up the ball of tape from the floor, and Louis settled back in his crouch, the plunger handle by his ear. Bob tossed the tape, and Louis again missed it by at least a foot. Bob shook his head.

"I can tell by the way you're standing," he said. "The tightness in your shoulders. The nervous twitch of your bat. You're not thinking about the ball . . . you're thinking that Mickey Mantle and Roger Maris are watching you. You're thinking about how embarrassing it will be if you swing and miss. You're thinking about everything except the one thing that you should be thinking about."

"Which is what?" Mickey asked, a smile on his face.

"The ball," Bob said. "There's nothing but the ball."

He picked up the tape and tossed it again. Louis missed again. But he was closer.

"Better," Bob said. "What did I hit last year, kid?"

Louis thought for a second. ".252."

"That's right. Which means that three out of every four times I came to the plate, I popped up or grounded to the shortstop or struck out. Three out of four times I failed."

He tossed the ball again. This time Louis nicked it, and it rolled to a stop near Bob's foot. He picked it up and weighed it in his hand.

"Everyone fails at baseball," he said. "Even Mickey and Roger. But if you keep working, people won't remember the pop flies and groundouts. They'll remember the home runs."

He tossed it again. This time Louis stared at the tape as if it were the only thing in the world, and the wood handle moved forward without Louis even realizing that he had made a conscious decision to swing. A sticky *thwack* rang around the room, and the ball of tape smacked against the far wall. Louis glanced down at the shaft of wood in his hands, confused.

"There you go," Bob said. "That's one out of four. Just like me."

Louis was quiet. He wanted to enjoy the moment.

"It's easy when kids aren't yelling at you," he finally said.

Bob raised one eyebrow. "If you think it's easier to hit in front of Mickey Mantle and Roger Maris than a bunch of kids . . . well, you're a better man than me."

"You listen to Bob," Roger said. "He's a smart man when he's not pretending to be a clown."

Louis nodded. "Yes, sir."

The men returned to the kitchen table and their card game, and Louis picked up the ball of tape as a souvenir. He made an excuse and left soon afterward so that he would be back home in time for dinner. It took almost two hours to get back to White Plains, but Louis didn't mind. He spent most of the trip staring at the seat in front of him and replaying that last swing in his head. It had felt so good when he finally hit the tape—clean and solid and natural. Every other time that Louis had gotten a hit, whether in Little League or gym class or the stickball games, it had felt like a cosmic accident. If you swung enough times, even with your eyes closed, you'd eventually hit something.

But this time had been different. This time he had done exactly what he wanted to do, and his stupid brain hadn't tried to sabotage him. There was obviously an enormous difference between a piece of tape tossed underhand and a real pitch in a real game, but Louis nevertheless felt good. For one brief moment he'd been a ballplayer.

CHAPTER TWELVE

Bottom of the Sixth

Ivan, the neighborhood bully, had pale skin and light-blue eyes that always looked watery. He wore short-sleeve collared shirts, even in the middle of the winter, and he never seemed to hang out with anyone his own age. Most afternoons he would wander the streets looking for targets, and kids would scatter like frightened deer the moment they saw him.

Ivan had caught Louis only once. It had been just a few weeks after Louis and his father had moved to White Plains, and Louis had been staring at the photographs in *Sports Illustrated* as he walked home from the baseball card store. Louis didn't realize that Ivan was nearby until the magazine was snatched from his grasp and a thick arm pulled him into a headlock.

"You got any money?" Ivan asked.

"No," Louis said, his voice straining through the headlock.

The arm tightened. "Don't lie to me."

"I swear."

The arm released Louis and shoved him into the side of a parked car. As Louis found his balance, Ivan waved the *Sports Illustrated* at him.

"Thanks for the magazine," he said.

That memory was playing in Louis's head as he rode over to Ivan's house. And as he leaned the bike against a tree in the yard and slowly walked up the driveway, every instinct in his brain was telling him to turn and run in the opposite direction. But what kept Louis's feet moving were the thousands and thousands of hours he had spent poring over his baseball cards. He wasn't going to give them up without a fight, which was why he forced himself up onto the porch and pressed his finger against the bell. When the front door finally opened, Louis's stomach jumped. But it wasn't Ivan—it was a short, thin woman in a blue print dress.

"Can I help you?" she asked, her voice barely above a whisper.

"I'm looking for Ivan," Louis said.

She opened the door a little wider. "Are you a friend?"

Louis paused. "Yes."

She smiled a warm smile. "I'm so glad. His friends never come here. Will you wait for just a second?"

"Sure," Louis said.

"Do you want a lemonade or something?"

"I'm okay," Louis said. "Thanks."

She disappeared into the house and Louis waited, his foot nervously tapping against the painted wood of the porch. After a minute or two Ivan emerged from the house and slammed the door behind him. He was wearing his usual short-sleeve collared shirt and a pair of khaki pants.

"What do you want?" he asked.

"I'm Louis. Bryce's stepbrother."

"I know who you are. What do you want?"

"Those baseball cards don't belong to Bryce," Louis said, trying to keep his tone firm. "They're mine."

Ivan shrugged. "Why would I care?"

Louis pointed at the bike, which was leaning against a tree on the lawn. "I'll give you the bike back. I just want the cards."

Ivan rolled his eyes. "I don't want the bike, dummy. That's why I traded it."

"You don't want the bike because you stole Joey Hammond's bike."

Ivan's hands tightened into fists. "Are you calling me a thief?"

"Joey's too scared to tell his parents," Louis said. "But I'm not."

"You're going to tell Joey's parents?" Ivan asked with a skeptical sneer.

"Nope. I'm going to go make a report at the police station. The bike is worth more than fifty bucks, so it's a felony. You'll end up at juvenile hall."

It was a total bluff. Louis knew that he would never be brave enough to walk into a police station, and even if he did, the officers would probably laugh him out of the building. Police officers had better things to worry about than kids and their little problems. And the part about juvenile hall had come from a threat that Mr. Wilson had made on an episode of *Dennis the Menace*—Louis wasn't even sure that a town like White Plains even had a juvenile hall.

Ivan was staring at him, and Louis tried to stare back and keep from shifting nervously. The only weapon he had was confidence, but his traitorous legs wanted to turn his body around and dash wildly down the street. A very long moment passed. And then Ivan looked away.

"Fine," he said. "I don't want your stupid cards anyway."

He turned and stalked into the house. Louis waited by the door for what seemed like five minutes, and just when he was starting to wonder if it was a trick, Ivan stepped outside and shoved the two boxes into his hand.

"Get out of here," he said. "And if you tell anyone about this, I'll find you every day after school this year."

Louis nodded and scurried off the porch. Joey's bike was leaning against the garage, and Louis grabbed it and walked it back to his house. He stashed the cards in his new hiding spot—under the winter blankets in the linen closet—and then rode the bike over to Joey's house. The bike was bright red with long handlebars and brakes that worked so well that you could skid to a stop.

Joey was a skinny kid with a short crew cut and huge ears who occasionally played stickball and was almost as bad as Louis. He was bouncing a basketball in his driveway as Louis rode up, and when he noticed the bike, his eyes got big.

"How'd you get my bike?" he asked.

"I found it on the street," Louis said. "I thought it was yours."

Joey reached out and touched the handlebar as if he wasn't sure whether or not he was dreaming. "Ivan took it."

"Maybe he got bored," Louis said. "Or maybe he's too dumb to ride it."

Joey laughed. "Well, thanks for bringing it back."

"No problem."

"You just moved here, right?"

"At the beginning of the summer."

"Are you going into seventh grade?"

"Yeah," Louis said.

"Me too."

They were silent for a moment, and Louis was just about to turn and leave when Joey glanced at his house. "You want to play some All-Star Baseball or something?"

"Sure," Louis said.

All-Star Baseball was a board game. You spun a wheel, and it told you whether you got a hit or struck out or something else. Louis preferred a brand-new game called Strat-O-Matic, which used dice and was much more complicated and realistic, but it was nice to be playing a game against somebody else. The afternoon passed quickly, and Louis was surprised when Joey's mother told him that it was time for dinner. Bryce was waiting for him on the front porch when he got home.

"Where's my bike?" he asked, his arms folded across his chest.

"Don't you mean Ivan's bike?" Louis asked as he walked past Bryce into the house.

Bryce muttered something and followed him into the dining room. Dinner was corned beef with gravy and mashed potatoes. Bryce was unusually quiet until he finished eating, and then he shoved his plate away from him and looked at his mother.

"My new bike is missing," he said.

"Oh, no," she said. "What happened?"

"It was in the garage this morning. And then Louis left and it disappeared."

She turned her head to Louis, her lips pursing. "Do you know anything about this?"

"When did Bryce get a new bike?" Louis asked.

"Don't change the subject," she said. "I asked you a question."

Louis ignored her and looked at his father. "Did you give Bryce a bike?"

His father carefully chewed and swallowed his food. He stared at Louis for a long moment before finally turning his attention to Bryce. "When did you get a new bike?"

"I traded for it," Bryce said.

"What did you trade?" Louis asked.

Bryce shifted uncomfortably in his seat. "Nothing."

Louis's father gave Bryce a skeptical look. "Someone just gave you a bike?"

"Maybe he borrowed it from someone and they took it back," Louis said. "Maybe that's what happened."

"I don't like the sound of this," his father said. "This sounds like stealing."

"I'm sure that Bryce wouldn't steal anything," his step-mother said.

Louis couldn't manage to keep a smile from pushing its way onto his face. His father caught him, and he turned and pointed at the stairs.

"Bryce and your stepmother and I are going to have a conversation," he said. "Go wait in your room."

Louis walked upstairs and closed the door to the bedroom as loudly as possible because he didn't want to be accused of eavesdropping. He also didn't want to gloat, but that was pretty hard because Louis had never seen Bryce get in real trouble. Occasionally, his father might say something when Bryce didn't finish his vegetables or take out the trash, but a big talk? The stern voice? Never.

Louis lay on his bed and opened his copy of *To Kill a Mockingbird.* Although he was supposed to finish the book by the start of school, so far he'd only managed to make it through the first few pages. His eyes aimlessly scanned the same paragraph over and over until the door swung open and Bryce stormed into the room. He glared at Louis and slammed the door.

"I can't play stickball for a week," he said. "And it's your fault."

Louis snorted. "How is it my fault? You stole my cards. And then you tried to get me in trouble."

"I hate your father. He never listens to me."

"Your mother never listens to me," Louis said.

Bryce opened the door and pointed out into the hallway. "Get out of my room!"

"Fine," Louis said.

He grabbed the pillow from his bed and stalked toward the door, but just before he crossed the threshold, he felt something red and hot rising in his chest. Bryce had never been anything but mean to Louis, and now he was pretending to be the victim, even though the fact he was in trouble was his own fault. It was ridiculous. Louis turned, threw his pillow at his bed, and folded his arms across his chest.

"You think I want to share a room with a jerk like you?" he asked, his voice almost a shout. "Nobody ever asked me if this was okay. Nobody asked me if I wanted to move to White Plains or go to a new school or make new friends. Nobody ever asked me anything!"

"I'm not a jerk," Bryce said. "You're a jerk."

"How am I a jerk? I've never done anything to you. But

you couldn't even let me tell Doug and Alex about the Yankees without ruining it."

The words exploded out of Bryce's mouth. "Because it's not fair! I'm older, but you get to go to all the Yankees games and take the train by yourself and spend the night in New York with your mother. And I'm stuck here playing stupid stickball."

For a long moment Louis was speechless. It had never occurred to him that Bryce might be jealous of *anything*—he was always confident to the point of being cocky. But as Louis thought about, it he realized that it made sense. After all, Bryce also loved baseball and the Yankees. And what kid wouldn't want to be a batboy? Sometimes in the daily grind of taking the train to the stadium or dragging a full cart of dirty underwear to the laundry room, Louis forgot how lucky he was, but as he stared into Bryce's angry eyes, he remembered how great it felt to be able to walk into that locker room. How great it felt to button his uniform.

"You like stickball," Louis finally said. "And you're really good at it."

"It's just a dumb kids' game."

"I'd give up being a batboy to be good at stickball."

"Really?"

Louis considered the question for a moment. "No."

"You never even ask me if I want to go to the games," Bryce said. "You never show me any of the stuff that you bring home. You never even tell me stories about the players."

"I'm sorry."

Bryce ignored him and flopped onto his bed. Louis stood rooted to the floor for a minute or two, thinking about the conversation. He couldn't help feeling a little guilty. Maybe

Bryce never made much of an effort to be nice to Louis, but Louis didn't make much of an effort to be nice to him, either. Bryce was right—Louis never found him free tickets or brought him anything from the ballpark or even tried to talk to him about baseball.

Louis went over to his sock drawer and rummaged around until he found a ball that he had hidden behind his underwear a few weeks earlier. He tossed it on the bed next to Bryce. It landed with a soft *thump*, and Bryce rolled over and glanced at it.

"What's that?" he asked.

"It's a game ball. It bounced into the dugout on a foul."

Bryce picked up the dirty ball and rolled it in his hand. His finger paused on the scrawl of black ink.

"Does that say 'Mickey Mantle'?" he asked, his eyes getting big.

"Yeah," Louis said. "I asked him to sign it."

Bryce kept staring at the ball. "What's Mickey like?"

"He's funny," Louis said. "He tells a lot of jokes and talks a lot. I think he knows that everyone's always looking at him, so he tries to put on a show."

"I hope he breaks the record."

"I want them both to break the record."

"I know you like Roger," Bryce said. "He's pretty good too."

Bryce gave the ball one long last look and then held it out to Louis as if it were a grenade or something else that might explode if it were dropped.

"Keep it," Louis said.

"What?"

"You should have it. Mickey's your favorite player."

Bryce glanced at the ball and then back at Louis.

"Thanks."

"You're welcome."

Louis picked the pillow up from the floor and settled onto his own bed. Bryce was still staring at him.

"Tell me a story," he said.

"What kind of story?"

"Something about the players. Something I couldn't read in the paper."

Louis pretended to think for a moment, but he knew exactly what he was going to say—he had wanted to tell someone about learning how to swing a bat since the moment it had happened.

"Well," he began, "this one time I went to Mickey and Roger's apartment . . ."

CHAPTER THIRTEEN

Top of the Seventh

School began the next week. Being a new kid was exactly as hard as Louis expected, and he tried to stay invisible and avoid the bullies. He had taught Strat-O-Matic baseball to Joey, who was the closest thing he had to a friend, and sometimes they would play at recess. The part of school that Louis was truly dreading was Parents' Day, which was coming in a few weeks. His father would have to work, and Louis knew he couldn't count on his mother, who hadn't bothered to visit him in White Plains—or even call—since the last time he'd seen her in New York, which meant that he would probably be the only kid without a parent. And that, Louis knew, would lead to attention from the other kids—and attention, at least in middle school, was always bad.

But Louis was generally in too good of a mood to worry about Parents' Day or get annoyed at his mother, because the Yankees were playing so well. On September 1 they had been a mere game and a half ahead of Detroit in the race for the pennant, but they swept the Tigers that weekend and began their usual early-autumn tear. Two weeks later, after massacring Washington, Cleveland, and Chicago, they were in first place by eleven and a half games, and the race was effectively over. Mickey and Roger were still blasting home runs at a blistering pace, and over those two torrid weeks Roger hit five and Mickey hit six. Roger now had 56 on the season and Mickey had 53—both within striking range of Babe Ruth's magic 60. Reporters were constantly roving the clubhouse like hungry wolves, and Roger was a nervous wreck. He even snapped at several umpires after bad calls, which was something that Louis had never seen him do before.

Although Mickey seemed to be dealing with the pressure better, he was fighting several injuries. He had pulled a muscle in his forearm, and it hurt him badly enough that he was constantly icing it in the dugout and locker room. But he kept hitting home runs anyway, and when the reporters asked him about the injury he would just wink and say, "It's shortening my swing."

On September 14 Louis got out of school late and rushed straight to the stadium. The Yankees had a doubleheader against the White Sox, and he arrived after most of the players had already gone outside to warm up. Roger was standing at his locker in the empty room and staring into a small mirror, one hand slowly rubbing the top of his scalp.

"Heya, Lucky," he said as Louis grabbed his uniform from the pile.

Louis took a few steps toward the locker. "You want me to find you a comb?"

Roger shook his head, an odd expression on his face. "I'm losing my hair, kid."

"Why?"

"Nerves, I guess."

Roger grabbed his cap from the top shelf and pulled it over his head as he headed for the tunnel. Louis changed as quickly as possible and was in the dugout by the national anthem. In the bottom of the first Mickey walked to load the bases with one out, but Yogi Berra, the next hitter, grounded to short. Although Mickey slid hard into second trying to break up the double play, Aparicio and Fox were too fast with the ball and the inning ended.

Louis ran Mickey's glove out to second base so that he wouldn't have to come back to the dugout before taking the field. Mickey was dusting himself off, his eyes aimlessly wandering the stands. Louis glanced at Mickey's pants and was surprised to notice a wet stain on his hip where he had slid. The stain was a rich, rusty color.

"I think you hurt yourself, Mr. Mantle," Louis said as Mickey took his glove.

Mickey glanced down. "Ah, shoot."

"Want me to tell Mr. Houk?"

"No." Mickey slid his hand into his glove. "Don't tell anyone. Just go back in the locker room and find me some bandages and clean pants, okay? I'll meet you in there after this inning."

Louis nodded and then sprinted back to the dugout. As he turned the corner into the tunnel that led to the locker room, Gabe stepped in his way.

"Where are you going?" he asked.

"Mickey tore his pants," Louis said. "I'm going to find him some new ones."

"Okay," Gabe said. "But get another bag of sunflower seeds while you're in there."

Louis dashed down the tunnel and into the locker room. He found a spare pair of uniform pants in the laundry room and grabbed bandages and first aid ointment from the trainer's closet. He had just returned to Mickey's locker with a few clean towels and a bucket of warm water when Mickey limped down the tunnel, his cleats clattering on the concrete floor.

"Thanks, kid," he said as he settled onto a bench.

He slowly peeled off his pants to reveal a bloodstained bandage covering his hip. The bandage was about the size of a cocktail napkin and was held in place by a few pieces of tape.

"What happened?" Louis asked.

Mickey prodded the bandage. "I've been sick all season, so I went to some quack doctor. He gave me a shot for my immune system. I guess it got infected."

"It looks pretty bad."

"Yeah," Mickey said. "And it feels worse than it looks."

Mickey slowly pulled the bandage away from his skin. The wound itself was red and angry, and it was surrounded by an ugly blue bruise. Louis handed Mickey a wet towel. He dabbed at the area, wincing every time the cloth touched his skin.

"Maybe you should take the rest of the game off," Louis said.

Mickey laughed. "In New York? With this record hanging over my head? They'd burn me at the stake, kid."

"Not if they knew you were hurt."

"I don't care if they cut my leg off. I ain't quitting. Not

when I'm this close to the Babe." Mickey paused and shook his head. "Can you imagine? Breaking his record? In this ballpark? After all the stuff people said about me, how I'll never be as good as Ruth or DiMaggio. It sure would be nice to be able to point to that record."

"Everyone loves you in New York," Louis said.

Mickey rolled his eyes. "Sure, they love me now. Do you know why? Because they've got Roger to root against. In this town it's not enough for someone to be succeeding. Someone has to be failing, too. It's like a comic book; for every hero they need a villain. That's just the way it is. And if you like the good things about this city—the excitement and the passion and the intensity—then you better learn to live with it."

"Does Roger love the good things about this city?"

Mickey glanced at Louis, his blue eyes empty. "You're a smart kid. You figure it out."

Mickey grabbed the first aid ointment, slathered it across his wound, and then slapped a fresh bandage on top. One minute and three pieces of tape later he was in the clean pants, and as he straightened his jersey he glanced at Louis.

"How do I look?" he asked.

"Like a million bucks," Louis said. It was something that his father used to say to his mother when he was trying to cheer her up.

Mickey smiled a tired smile. "Well, I feel like a bum nickel. But it will have to do."

The Yankees lost the first game of the doubleheader 8-3. Although Louis expected Mickey to sit out the second game, he started in center field. Going into the ninth inning the Yankees led 3-1, but Luis Arroyo, the Yankees reliever, gave up a leadoff single. He then got two quick outs before walking Floyd Robinson to put men at first and second. The next batter, Minnie Minoso, hit a sinking line drive to right field. Roger ran to his left and had a chance to catch the ball, but it glanced off the heel of his glove for his eighth error of the season. Although Mickey was backing up the play and held Minoso to a single, a run scored to make it 3-2. As Roger trudged back to his position, his cap pulled low over his eyes, scattered boos trickled down from the stands.

"Listen to that," Houk said to nobody in particular on the bench. "That guy's hit fifty-six homers, we're up eleven games in the standings, and those idiots are booing."

The booing only intensified when Sherm Lollar and Al Smith hit consecutive singles, and by the time Jim Landis finally grounded out to short, the White Sox were leading 4-3. Roger ran in from right field, sticking close to the first-base line, and Louis could hear a few catcalls from the fans. Roger was a dozen feet from the dugout when he abruptly stopped. He slowly turned toward the crowd, his mouth moving but his words lost in the hubbub of the ballpark. A man in the front row said something back, and Roger pulled the glove from under his arm and gently tossed it to him. A moment later he was back in the dugout. Mickey was staring at him.

"What the heck did you do that for?" he asked.

Roger shrugged. "That guy said that it was an easy catch. So I told him that he should take my glove and play out there if he thought it was so easy."

He sat on the bench and buried his head in his hands. A long moment passed. And then he slammed his fist against the blue wood and turned his gaze down the dugout. His eyes stopped on Louis.

"Lucky," he called.

Louis scurried down the dugout to his side. "Yes, Mr. Maris."

"I need that glove. Will you go up in the stands and try to get it back?"

"Sure thing."

"It's important. Trade a bat. Trade ten bats. Whatever that guy wants."

There were already two outs in the bottom of the ninth by the time Louis made his way from the dugout to the front row of the first-base stands. The man who had caught the glove was short and stout with thick, curly hair that covered his ears. He was wearing a white shirt and an ugly brown jacket that matched his brown pants.

"I ain't giving it back," he said before Louis even opened his mouth. "Roger tossed it to me, so it's mine. Fair and square."

"Mr. Maris wants to know if you'll trade him. A bat for his glove."

The man shook his head, his black curls bouncing. "Cash or nothing."

"Roger and Mickey will sign the bat. Two guys in the middle of the greatest home run chase of all time."

"A lot of people have bats. A glove is different. It's special."

"Come on, Tony," someone in the stands said. "Give the kid a break."

Tony turned around, suddenly angry, and tapped his chest. "Maybe it's time *I* got a break, huh?"

Louis tried not to sound desperate. "Two bats. And a ball signed by Whitey Ford."

Tony shook his head. "Listen, kid. I saw Roger once down on Mulberry Street. He was going into a restaurant, and when I asked him for an autograph, he told me to scram. So now I'm telling you and I'm telling him . . . I ain't doing him no favors."

The crowd was starting to mutter, and Tony reached into his pocket and pulled out a slip of paper and a pen. He quickly scrawled something on the paper and shoved it into Louis's hand.

"You tell Roger I want this or nothing," he said. "Now beat it."

Louis heard a ball smack into a mitt, and he turned his head just in time to see the umpire raise his arm. Clete Boyer had struck out to end the game. The man with the glove pushed his way past Louis to the aisle, and Louis stood amid the departing crowd for a long moment, dejected. Roger had asked him for a favor, and he had failed. But the man hadn't wanted the balls or bats. What else was he supposed to offer?

Louis eventually hopped the small barrier that led to the field and trotted down the first-base line to the dugout. Back in the clubhouse a few reporters were surrounding Roger's locker, and Louis waited on the other side of the room. He was so preoccupied with worrying about how he was going to break the bad news to Roger that he didn't notice that Nathan Scully and two other reporters had cornered him until Nathan grabbed him by the scruff of his jersey.

"Hey, kid," Nathan said. "Long time, no see."

Louis tried to squirm away from Nathan, but the reporter's grip was too strong. "What do you want?"

"One question," Nathan said. "Why did Mickey go into the clubhouse in the first game?"

"I don't know."

"Come on. I heard you were back there."

"He tore his pants when he was sliding," Louis said. "I had to get him new ones."

Nathan raised a skeptical eyebrow. "Tore his pants?"

"It happens," Louis said. "Especially when the infield is dry."

Louis twisted again, and this time he separated himself from Nathan's firm hand. He scurried down the hall to the laundry room, where he helped the assistant equipment manager load the washers with soiled jerseys and pants, and by the time he was finished most of the reporters had dashed away to file their stories before their deadlines. Roger was sitting in front of his locker wearing a coat and tie.

"I'm sorry," Louis said. "I didn't get the glove."

Roger's blue-gray eyes flicked up. He looked exhausted.

"He didn't want the balls or bats," Louis continued. "He just gave me this . . ."

Louis held out the piece of paper. Roger glanced at it and his eyes widened.

"Five hundred bucks!" he said. "That's ridiculous. I could buy a color television for that. Or a pickup truck."

"Don't you have another glove?" Louis asked.

"I've got plenty of gloves. But that one was special."

"Why?"

"I know it sounds stupid, but that glove was almost as lucky as you. Remember how I started this year in an awful slump?"

"Sure," Louis said. Roger had struggled for the first thirty games of the season, which made his run at the record even more remarkable.

"Well, I tried everything. Spat on my bats, went to church, kissed a black cat, carried a four-leaf clover. Everything. But I just kept hitting worse and worse. Finally, we were in Cleveland on our off day, and one of my cousins came to visit. We were playing catch and joking around, and he told me that he wanted to trade gloves so that he could tell his kids that he was using real professional equipment.

"Anyway, I didn't like the glove I had been using much, so I gave it to him. And it turned out that his glove felt pretty good. So the next day I tried it in the field, and that's when I began my streak. I hit three home runs in the next three games and twenty-three in the next thirty-five."

"That doesn't sound stupid," Louis said. "Some things are just lucky."

"Well, it doesn't matter now," Roger said. He shook his head as he took a slow breath. "It's gone."

He rolled up the piece of paper, tossed it on the floor, and slowly made his way out of the locker room. Louis waited until he had disappeared before picking up the paper and carefully spreading it out against a bench. It was a receipt from a dry cleaning store in New York, and "$500" was scrawled on the back in a looping hand. Louis gave the receipt a long look and then shoved it in his pocket. He wasn't quite sure why he wanted to keep it, but Louis wasn't ready to let Roger's lucky glove go without a fight. And the little slip of paper was the only clue that he had.

CHAPTER FOURTEEN

Bottom of the Seventh

The wound in Mickey's side got infected and he ended up in the hospital with a 104-degree fever. Although he somehow managed to keep playing, his power was sapped, and he remained stuck on 53 home runs. Yet Roger, despite the missing glove, kept on going. He hit two home runs in Detroit to get to 58, only two behind Babe Ruth, and Louis's optimism soared. But then Roger could barely get the ball out of the infield in a doubleheader against Baltimore on September 19, and Louis spent a sleepless night thinking about all of the things he should have said to the fat man in the stands.

The next day, September 20, the sporting world turned its full attention to Baltimore. Every baseball fan and newspaper in the country was asking the same question: Could Roger Maris, a man who had entered the season with only 97 career home runs, somehow hit two more and match the immortal Babe Ruth's record in 154 games? Louis begged his father to take him on the train to Baltimore to watch the game in person, but he knew that he was wasting his time. His father never did anything that spontaneous—and certainly not on a Wednesday night.

Louis and Bryce and Louis's father therefore watched the black-and-white broadcast of the game on television. Louis could tell by the way the spectators were dressed that it was a chilly, wet night. The camera briefly focused on the stadium's flags, which showed that the wind was blowing in from right field, and Louis's heart sank. Roger was a dead pull hitter, which meant that any ball he hit would have to cut through the teeth of that gale.

In the top of the first Roger came up with Bobby Richardson on first base. He got a good pitch to hit and drove it toward right, but it was too low and Earl Robinson caught it well before the warning track. Louis closed his eyes and groaned. Roger now had three or maybe four at bats to hit two home runs against a driving wind. It seemed impossible.

Louis was still depressed when Roger again came to the plate in the top of the third. There was one out and nobody on base. Milt "Gimpy" Pappas, a tall pitcher with excellent control, was on the mound. His first pitch, a fastball, was inside.

"He's thrown nothing but fastballs to Roger," Louis said.

"Maybe he wants Roger to break the record," his father said. "I read in the paper that a lot of the ballplayers are angry about the commissioner and his asterisk."

Louis tried to smile, but he was too nervous. Pappas was already in his windup. It looked like another fastball, and just as Roger started his swing, the television picture got fuzzy. As Louis leaped toward the antenna, the image suddenly sharpened. The camera was swinging toward the outfield, and Louis caught a glimpse of the 380-foot marker just before the ball disappeared into the teeming crowd.

"Fifty-nine," Bryce said.

Louis danced around the couch, but then his nerves overwhelmed him, and he settled back onto the floor. The tension was unbearable. All Roger needed was one good swing, and the pushy reporters and the booing and everything else would all be irrelevant. Roger and the Babe would forever be tied, and the commissioner wouldn't get to use his stupid asterisk.

The rest of the game felt like an eternity. Louis suffered while waiting for Roger to come to the plate and then suffered much more when he finally did. In the top of the fourth Roger hit a long foul ball against Dick Hall and then struck out on a breaking pitch in the dirt. In the seventh he smashed another foul, this one just ten feet away from a record-tying home run. The crowd sighed and Louis collapsed in a nervous heap. On the next pitch Hall left a fastball over the plate. Roger swung hard and hit it squarely, and for a second Louis thought that he had tied the record—Louis had seen that swing dozens of times over the season, and every time it had produced a home run. But the ball got caught in the wind, and Earl Robinson caught it on the edge of the warning track.

And so everything came down to Roger's last at bat. It was the top of the ninth, the Yankees leading 4-2 and about to clinch the pennant, and Baltimore's manager brought in knuckleballer Hoyt Wilhelm. The wind was raging and the knuckleball was dancing, and on the first pitch Roger tried to check his swing and bounced a slow grounder foul. He stepped out of the box and wiped his forehead. Even through the fuzzy television set Louis could feel his anxiety.

Roger dug in, and the next pitch fluttered to the plate. Once again Roger tried to check his swing, and once again he hit a slow grounder. But this time the ball stayed fair, and Wilhelm grabbed it and stepped on first. The race was over. Roger Maris had hit 59 home runs in 154 games. One fewer than Babe Ruth.

Louis numbly watched the bottom of the ninth inning, and when Baltimore went down in order and the Yankees ran on the field to celebrate, he stood up and slowly walked upstairs to his room. He was obviously glad that the Yankees had won the pennant, but the Yankees almost always won the pennant, and they had entered the game up ten games in the standings with ten games to go.

No, the story of the day was Roger. Louis had watched enough baseball in his short life to know that what Roger had been doing was special—Louis might live to be a hundred and never see another player standing at the plate with a chance to break Ruth's record. Why couldn't that foul ball have been just a dozen feet to the left? Why couldn't the wind have died or the bat have been a fraction of an inch lower or any of the other hundreds of tiny things in a game—or a season—that could mean the difference between 59 home runs and 60. It was just bad luck.

And that was why Louis knew that he would never forgive himself for not being able to return Roger's glove. Louis wasn't superstitious by nature, but most baseball players were. And Louis understood why. Baseball was a sport of highs and lows, good streaks and bad streaks, and luck was as rational an explanation as anything for why a grounder to the shortstop might be an inning-ending double play and a grounder a dozen feet to the left might score the winning run. Roger obviously believed in luck; maybe losing the glove had just affected his confidence, or maybe there really was something special about that glove. Either way, Roger had asked Louis for a favor and Louis had failed. He had failed as a batboy and a fan and a friend.

Louis was still beating himself up when Bryce came upstairs for bed. He leaned against his dresser, his eyes locked on Louis, and Louis braced himself for a snide remark.

"I'm sorry about Roger," Bryce said.

Louis's mouth fell open. "What?"

"He was really close. I thought he was going to do it after he hit the first one. But it's okay. It will still be a record if he does it in one hundred and sixty-two games."

"You think?" Louis asked, still trying to contain his surprise.

"Sure. Maybe it's not the same as what the Babe did, but it's not Roger's fault that the commissioner added games to the schedule. The book says, 'single season record.' It doesn't say, 'record for a hundred and fifty-four games.'"

"Maybe it will next year," Louis said.

In the silence that followed, Louis tried to figure out why Bryce was acting so friendly. The most likely explanation was that aliens had kidnapped the real Bryce and replaced him with a robot programmed to be nice. Or maybe this was Bryce's way of thanking him for the Mickey Mantle ball. Either way, Louis decided that he was going to take advantage of the moment. He rarely got a chance to talk about baseball with anyone outside of the Yankee locker room.

"He lost his lucky glove," Louis said.

"Who?" Bryce asked. "Roger?"

"He tossed it in the stands and he asked me to go get it and the guy wouldn't give it back. Maybe that's what happened tonight with the wind and the foul ball."

"Why wouldn't the guy give it back?"

Louis shrugged. "He wanted five hundred bucks."

"Didn't he want Roger to break the record?"

Louis almost smiled. Bryce was the most superstitious kid in the neighborhood—it made perfect sense that he would believe in a lucky glove. "I guess not."

"You need to get that glove back," Bryce said firmly.

"How?"

"I don't know. Find the guy. Give him some money. Or make him give it to you."

"I don't know how to find him," Louis said. "And he's not going to give me the glove anyway. Not unless I magically find five hundred dollars under my pillow."

Bryce was staring at Louis, his eyes slightly narrow. After a long moment, he shrugged.

"I'll help you," he said. "But I want you to take me to a game."

It took Louis only a second to consider the offer. Bryce was a smooth talker, which would be valuable if they actually managed to find the man with the glove, and it would be much less intimidating to wander around New York with a partner.

"Okay," Louis said. "But I still don't think we can find that glove."

Bryce smiled his trademark cocky smile. "Don't worry," he said. "We'll figure it out."

Because of school Bryce and Louis had to wait until Saturday to start their search. The more Louis thought about it, the more impossible their quest seemed. There were eight million people in New York, and their only real clue was the dry cleaning receipt. But Bryce wouldn't be discouraged, and that Saturday he told his mother that he and Louis needed to go to the Natural History Museum for a school project. He even managed to wheedle five dollars out of her for food and train tickets.

According to the receipt, the dry cleaner was on Mulberry Street, which was located near the very bottom of Manhattan in the heart of Little Italy. Louis became even more convinced that they were on a wild-goose chase when they emerged from the subway station and were nearly knocked over by hundreds of people storming in every direction. Restaurants and pizza parlors and cafés and grocery stores lined the street, and even the pavement seemed to be vibrating with the insistent energy of a beehive.

"We'll never find him," Louis said, staring forlornly at the hubbub.

"Sure we will," Bryce said. "A kid in my class is Italian, and his father says that everyone knows everyone in Little Italy."

"I think that's just an expression," Louis said.

Rocca's Dry Cleaning, the store from the receipt, was two blocks from the subway station. Louis paused outside the store, wondering if they should come up with some sort of plan, but Bryce pushed his way through the glass door, and

Louis reluctantly followed. The store smelled like starch and static, and thousands of suits and dresses were hanging on a rotating metal rack that circled the counter before disappearing into a dark room in the back. A thin woman with a long nose and hair the color of pine tar was standing behind the counter.

"Last name?" she asked as they entered.

Bryce handed her the receipt. She glanced at it and then put her hands on her hips.

"Are you boys trying to waste my time?" she asked. "There's no name on this receipt. And the order's already been picked up."

"We're looking for a guy," Bryce said as Louis tried to make himself invisible. "A fat guy named Tony."

The woman smiled, revealing a huge set of front teeth. "A fat guy named Tony? In Little Italy? There are probably a thousand of them."

"He really likes the Yankees. Thick, curly hair. He was wearing a brown suit."

She furrowed her brow. "An ugly brown suit? Like someone threw up a carpet?"

"Yeah."

She hit a button next to the cash register, and the clothes began to move on the rack. The clattering from the hangers sounded like the wheels of hundreds of toy trains. She hit the button again, and as the rack slowed to a stop, she pulled out a suit.

"This ugly?" she asked.

Louis took a close look. He couldn't be positive, but it seemed to be exactly the shade of hideous brown that he remembered from the ballpark.

"I think so," he said.

She glanced at the slip and then back at him, her thick eyebrows raised. "You know, I'm not supposed to give out the names of customers."

For a long moment Louis was confused. Why would she go to the trouble of finding the brown suit and then refuse to give him the name? And then suddenly it occurred to him; she might give him the name, but not for free.

"Do you like the Yankees?" Louis asked. "I can get you tickets."

She shrugged. "Baseball's boring."

Louis and Bryce exchanged a stunned look. Bryce was the first to be able to form a sentence. "Is that your son?" he asked, pointing at a small photo next to the cash register.

"Yeah."

"Does he like baseball?"

"Sure," she said.

Bryce reached into his jacket pocket and pulled out the Mickey Mantle ball that Louis had given to him. He carried it everywhere.

"This is a signed ball," he said. "Mickey Mantle. You can have it for your son if you tell me the name on that slip."

She examined the ball, her eyes squinted suspiciously, and then glanced down at the receipt on the plastic bag covering the suit.

"Tony Palazzo," she said. "200 Grand Street. Apartment 302. I think it's above DiPalo's Dairy."

Bryce turned and dashed for the door, and Louis bobbed his head at the woman before straining to catch up. They paused to ask a few people on the street for directions, and five minutes later they were standing in front of a battered brick apartment building. DiPalo's dairy indeed occupied the bottom floor, and the smell of cheese and fresh bread bathed the sidewalk. Bryce rang the buzzer, and the intercom crackled to life.

"Yeah?" a voice said.

Bryce held his hand over the microphone. "Is that him?"

"Maybe," Louis said. "I can't tell."

Bryce removed his hand. "We've got a package for Mr. Palazzo."

The door buzzed open, and they stepped into the building. The stairwell was dank and smelled of mildew. Apartment 302 was on the third floor, and a man wearing khakis and a stained white T-shirt was standing in the doorway. Louis was both relieved and amazed to realize that it was the right guy.

"Where's my package?" Tony asked. His gaze moved from Bryce to Louis, and his eyes narrowed. "Hey, you're the kid from the ballpark."

"We want to trade for the glove," Bryce said.

"I told your friend already. I ain't trading."

"You told him you'd sell it for five hundred bucks."

Tony's mouth curled in a skeptical sneer. "You've got five hundred bucks?"

"We'll give you two hundred tomorrow," Bryce said.

"Two hundred ain't five hundred."

Tony started to close the door, but Bryce stepped forward to block him. "Do you read the newspaper, Mr. Palazzo?"

"What's that got to do with anything?"

"Imagine this," Bryce said. "Star baseball player throws his lucky glove into the stands. Local man catches it and demands five hundred bucks. Star baseball player just misses tying Babe Ruth's record."

"That's pretty interesting," Louis said. "I bet a lot of people would want to hear a story like that."

"Sure," Bryce said. "I bet there would be so many report-ers in this hall that you couldn't get to the stairs."

Tony was silent for a long moment, his dark eyes locked on Bryce.

"What do you want?" he finally asked.

"It's a fair deal," Bryce said. "Two hundred bucks for the glove."

"Fine."

"We'll bring the money tomorrow."

Tony just grunted and slammed the door. As they started down the stairs, Louis gave Bryce a skeptical look.

"How are we going to get two hundred bucks?" he asked.

"I don't know," Bryce said. "But we've got twenty-four hours to figure it out."

On the long train ride home Bryce was giddy from their successful adventure. Louis did his best to play along, but he was preoccupied with the events of the day. They had been incredibly lucky. And maybe that was the point; maybe some of that same luck would help Roger if they actually returned the glove. Louis knew that it sounded crazy—like witchcraft or something. But he was willing to try almost anything that might help Roger Maris hit 61 home runs.

CHAPTER FIFTEEN

Top of the Eighth

Louis and Bryce agonized over how to find the money. They had a combined fifty-four dollars in cash, which Louis had been saving for a framed Yankees replica pennant and Bryce had been saving for roller skates, but that still left them 146 dollars short. They could try getting a loan from their parents or taking up a collection around the neighborhood, but they both knew that a hundred and fifty bucks was too much money. The kids would want something big in return, and their parents would demand a reason—which would probably mean explaining that they had been sneaking around New York City.

And so there was only one option. Late that Saturday afternoon Louis put his cards in his backpack and rode with Bryce down to Al's Collectables on Main Street. As Louis slowly unloaded his collection onto the counter, he reminded himself why he was doing what he was doing. He loved everything about his cards—owning them and trading them and studying them—but ultimately the cards were just a record of real life. They weren't life itself.

At that moment Louis finally realized how much being a batboy had changed him. He had once seen baseball as a game purely of numbers, but over the last few months Louis had come to realize that *how* people got those numbers was ultimately more interesting. It was like the difference between someone who collected stamps from foreign countries and someone who actually traveled the world. And that's why Louis knew that he would do anything to get Roger's glove back—including selling his collection. He wanted to be more than just a collector; he wanted to be part of something that he would remember for the rest of his life.

Unfortunately, Louis wasn't exactly sure how much his collection was worth. In stores you paid roughly a penny a card; Topps, for example, sold cards in packs of six for a nickel. But the moment you opened the pack, the value of the cards changed. You couldn't get any money at all for most cards at a place like Al's Collectables. They only wanted stars or old cards or cards with a mistake on the photograph or in the information on the back. The more rare the card, the more valuable it was.

Louis had therefore sorted his collection into four groups. The first group contained the worthless cards, which he had left at home. In the second group were the cards with some value—good players in interesting years. The third group contained the valuable cards that Louis didn't mind losing, generally cards with misprints or star players who Louis didn't like. Finally, the fourth group consisted of the untouchables, the cards that Louis had never considered trading to anyone, ever.

Al, the owner of the store, was a quiet man with a thick mustache and horn-rimmed glasses. When he finished adding up the value of the second and third group, he looked at Louis.

"Ninety-two dollars," he said.

"Come on," Bryce said. "It's got to be more than that."

Al shrugged apologetically. "That's the best I can do."

Louis stared at the stack of cards on the counter. It seemed impossible that in all of his years of careful collecting, with all of the great trades that he had made, that the bulk of his collection would be worth only ninety-two dollars. But it was what it was. He carefully spread his untouchable cards across the counter, a sick feeling in his stomach.

"Add these up too," he said.

Al sorted them deliberately, making a few notes on a plain sheet of paper. Louis nervously clutched the edge of the counter as Al did the math.

"Sixty," Al said.

Louis quickly added the numbers in his head. Ninety-two plus sixty plus the fifty-four that he and Bryce already had . . . the total was two hundred and six. Just enough to pay Tony.

"Okay," Louis said. "I'll take it in cash."

Al carefully counted out the money from the register, and Louis stuffed the wad into his front pocket. He knew that he should be excited that they would be able to buy back the lucky glove, but it felt as if there was a big hole in the center of his chest where his heart should be. He quickly turned and started toward the door, Bryce trailing behind him.

"I'll let you keep one," Al said behind him.

Louis stopped and slowly turned around. "What?"

Al spread the cards from the fourth group across the counter. "You pick, Louis. Whichever one you want."

Louis slowly retraced his steps, his eyes locked on the cards. He knew which card he should choose—the Topps Mickey Mantle card from 1952 was already considered the most valuable card for any player who had been on the field since the Second World War. But that wasn't where his eye landed.

"I want Roger Maris," he said. "1961."

Louis and Bryce decided that their parents would find it too suspicious if they returned to New York City together, so Louis went alone to Mulberry Street on Sunday. Tony somehow managed to be even more surly, and he counted every nickel of the two hundred dollars before reluctantly handing over the glove. The Yankees returned from their road trip the following morning, but Louis wasn't assigned to unpack the trucks because of school. The next game was against Baltimore on Tuesday, September 26. Halfway through dinner on Monday night Louis looked at his father.

"I want to take Bryce to the game tomorrow," he said. "The clubhouse man told me that I could get a free ticket for a friend."

His father and his stepmother exchanged a surprised look.

"Sure," his father said. "Is that okay with you, Bryce?"

"Of course," Bryce said as if the question was ridiculous—which, to be fair, it was.

So Louis and Bryce took the train together to the stadium after school on Tuesday. Fans weren't allowed in the park yet, but one of the clubhouse guys let Bryce sneak inside so that he could watch the players warm up. Louis went into the locker room, the glove hidden in a shopping bag, and changed into his uniform. He kept his eye on Roger's locker, and when most of the players had taken the field, he wandered over and carefully tucked the glove next to Roger's cleats.

"What's that?" a voice asked.

Louis glanced up, nervous. It was Mickey.

"A glove," Louis said.

"I know it's a glove," Mickey said. "Where did you get it?"

"It's the one that Mr. Maris tossed into the stands."

Mickey gave Louis a long look and then shouted across the locker room. "Hey, Rog. Get out here!"

As Louis stood and took a few big steps away from the locker, Roger emerged from the trainer's room.

"What's up, Mick?" he asked.

"Lucky got your glove back."

"What?" Roger crossed the room to his locker. Mickey was pointing at the glove, and Roger picked it up and carefully turned it in his hands before looking at Louis. "How did you get this?"

"I traded with the guy who had it," Louis said, shifting nervously under Roger's steady gaze.

"Why?"

The words came in a rush. "Because you have fifty-nine home runs and there are only five games left and I thought that you could use some luck."

For a long moment Roger and Mickey just stared at him. Roger had a strange smile on his face, a smile that almost looked sad around his eyes.

"This might be the nicest thing anyone's ever done for me," he finally said.

Mickey playfully nudged Louis in the ribs. "Quick, ask him for something," he said. "While the big ape is feeling all soft."

Roger was staring down at the glove again. "How did you get it?"

"My stepbrother Bryce helped me," Louis said. "I was hoping that maybe you and Mr. Mantle would say hi to him."

Roger looked at Mickey. "That seems more than fair. What do you say?"

Mickey clapped Louis on the back. "Sure," he said. "But I think you're getting a bum deal, kid. You should have asked for a heck of a lot more than that."

Roger put on his cleats and then the three of them walked down the tunnel and out of the dugout together. Louis's eyes scanned the stands. It was only half an hour before the game, but the stadium was almost empty—it was going to be a quiet night. Bryce was hanging over the barrier just to the outfield side of the dugout, his eyes locked on a few Yankees playing catch.

"There he is," Louis said, pointing.

Roger and Mickey ambled over to Bryce, Louis trailing them by a few steps. Bryce noticed them when they were only a few feet away. He stiffened as if someone had slid ice down his back.

"My friend Louis says that you helped him find my lucky glove," Roger said.

Louis had never seen Bryce speechless. It was funny, actually. His face went white and his eyes were wide and unblinking. Although he managed to nod, it clearly took a huge effort.

"I sure appreciate it," Roger said. He pointed at the ball in Bryce's hand. "Would you like us to sign that for you?"

Bryce stared down at his hand as if he had never seen it before and then thrust the ball at Roger. Louis stepped forward with a pen. When Mickey finished signing, he tossed the ball back to Bryce, one of his playful smiles on his face.

"I better hear you hollering from the stands during the game," he said. "Okay?"

Bryce finally found his voice. "Yes, sir."

Roger and Mickey both shook hands with him and then jogged to the outfield to begin warming up. Louis leaned against the edge of the stands and pretended to watch them, but his eyes kept flickering to his stepbrother. Most kids would have been jumping around, their mouths moving at a million miles a minute, but Bryce was still frozen. Louis recognized something in his expression. It was both strange and wonderful to meet someone you'd only seen on television or a baseball diamond—proof that even your heroes were made of flesh and blood.

At that moment Louis finally realized that he and Bryce did have something in common. Maybe Bryce was older and better at sports, but when faced with Roger Maris and Mickey Mantle, he had been just as speechless as Louis. It had never occurred to Louis that his stepbrother might love the Yankees as much as he did. In fact, it had never occurred to Louis that *anyone* might love the Yankees as much as he did. But clearly Bryce shared his passion, and Louis wondered if they had the same reasons. When Louis watched baseball he felt as if he was watching the world as it ought to be—men from wildly different backgrounds performing incredibly difficult tasks for a common cause.

And the reason that Louis loved the Yankees so much was that they were the absolute pinnacle of the sport. Over the course of Louis's short life they had achieved remarkable things: seven championships, a perfect game in the World Series, and a never-ending parade of players who graduated from pinstripes to the Hall of Fame. It wasn't just that they won—it was the way they won: great hitting, clutch pitching, solid fielding, smart baserunning. Maybe life wasn't perfect, but the Yankees almost always were.

Perhaps, Louis thought, that was the real reason he had been so obsessed with the home run chase. It sometimes felt as if nothing had gone right at home or at school since his mother moved to New York the previous spring, but his chance to be a batboy and Roger's pursuit of Babe Ruth's record had been absolutely magical. And maybe Bryce felt the same way—maybe the Yankees and baseball were a way to distract him from what had happened to his father in Korea.

"I bet Roger hits a home run tonight," Bryce said, interrupting Louis's thoughts. "I bet this is the night he ties the Babe."

"I hope so," Louis said. "It would be pretty cool to be here when it happens."

Bryce glanced at the growing crowd in the right-field stands. "Sometimes I think about what it would be like to catch the ball."

"I'd want to keep it," Louis said. "But I'd probably give it to Roger."

"So would I," Bryce said.

They quietly watched Roger and Mickey lazily play catch in the outfield. Their motions were smooth and relaxed, but the ball was snapping out of their hands. Sometimes Louis felt like he would be happy if he could just sit in the stadium and watch them warm up forever.

"I think I saw your mom," Bryce said after a long pause.

Louis's head swung around. "What?"

"In the concourse. I wasn't positive, so I followed her for a while." Bryce pointed across the diamond toward a section behind third base. "She's over there."

Louis stared, his eyes squinting with the effort. A woman with long brown hair was sitting alone, but at this distance it was impossible to tell if it really was his mother.

"You want me to get her to come over here or something?" Bryce asked.

"No," Louis said. "But thanks."

He pushed himself away from the stands and slowly trotted back to the dugout. The game began just after eight. In the bottom of the first, as Roger strode to the plate with a chance to tie the Babe, the crowd rose to its feet. Louis guessed that the stands were only a third full, but it still sounded as if the park was packed. Roger swung at the first pitch and hit a sharp single into center field. As the crowd settled back down, Mickey drew a walk on five pitches. When he got to first base he gestured to the dugout.

"Go find out what he wants," Mr. Houk said to Louis.

Louis sprinted out to Mickey's side. His face was pale, and his lips were a strange shade of blue. "It's no good," he said. "Tell Skip that I've gotta come out."

Louis relayed the information back to Mr. Houk, and

Hector Lopez jogged onto the field to pinch-run. Mickey slowly walked back to the dugout, neither acknowledging the cheers of the crowd nor making eye contact with the other players, and disappeared into the tunnel that led to the clubhouse. A minute later Yogi Berra hit an easy fly to left for the final out of the inning, and Louis trotted onto the field with Roger's glove.

"What's wrong with Mickey?" Roger asked.

"I don't know," Louis said. "He looked sick."

Roger shook his head, his mouth a tight line. "He needs to take better care of himself. We're going to need him in the Series."

The Orioles scored two runs in the top of the second, and Roger came up again in the bottom of the third with two outs and nobody on base. The Orioles pitcher was Fat Jack Fisher, which was a funny nickname because he wasn't very fat. Roger took a couple of deliberate practice swings and then dug into the batter's box. The crowd was once again on its feet, but Louis was so focused on Roger that the noise was just a buzzing in the background.

Fat Jack started his windup, and the ball streaked toward the plate. Roger shifted his weight forward, his swing compact, his balance perfect. After the *crack* of the bat he stayed in the box for an extra second, his chin tilted up as his eyes tracked the white streak against the night sky. And then, just as the ball banged off a seat in the upper deck of right field and Roger Maris tied Babe Ruth with 60 home runs in a single season, he began his deliberate trot around the bases.

The dugout and the ballpark erupted into bedlam. Louis

wanted to celebrate with the players, but he was afraid of being crushed. Instead he kept his eyes on the ball, which had bounced back onto the field next to Earl Robinson, the Orioles right fielder. Earl picked it up and tossed it toward the Yankee dugout, and Louis dashed out to retrieve it.

"Way to keep your head," Mr. Houk said when Louis returned to the dugout. "Put it in my office, okay?"

Louis nodded and ran down the tunnel. As he skidded into the locker room, he noticed a lonely shape dressed only in underwear hunched on one of the benches. It was Mickey—in all of the excitement Louis had completely forgotten about him. Mickey looked gaunt, and his underwear couldn't conceal the faint outline of the bulky bandage on his hip. He turned his red eyes to Louis.

"Was that cheering the sound of Roger hitting sixty?" he asked.

"Yes, sir."

Mickey slowly nodded his head. "Good for him. I'm glad someone finally caught that fat—" He stopped abruptly and glanced at Louis. "It's been a long season, kid. A very long season."

"Are you okay, Mr. Mantle?"

"I'm sick as a dog."

"Is it your hip?"

"I've put a lot of living on this body. I guess it's starting to quit on me."

"You're only twenty-nine years old," Louis said.

Mickey shrugged. "Sure. But my dad died at thirty-nine."

They were silent for a moment, and then Mickey smiled a shadow of one of his mischievous smiles.

"Go back to the dugout and celebrate with the boys," he said. "You shouldn't be in here listening to me howl at the moon."

Louis dashed into Mr. Houk's office with the ball, and just as he returned to the clubhouse, he heard the sound of cleats in the tunnel. Roger stepped into the room, and Mickey pushed himself to his feet, his hand extended.

"It's the hero of the hour," he said. "Congratulations."

The two men shook hands, their eyes avoiding each other.

"I'm glad that you tied the Babe," Mickey said as their hands separated. "But I expect you to break that record before this season ends. And I don't care what that fool commissioner says. A record's a record. It don't matter how many games."

"Thanks, Mick."

Mickey flicked his head at the tunnel. "It must feel good to hear everyone cheering for you, huh?"

Roger shrugged. "If I pretend not to care when they boo, can I really care when they cheer?"

"It's your choice," Mickey said. "But it's a lot more fun when you care."

"I don't know," Roger said. "I've learned this season that you can't do things for the crowd. You've got to do them for yourself and the people you love. Because they're the ones who will be around when things go bad."

In the silence that followed, Louis thought of the lonely woman in the stands, and he knew that he had to find out if it really was his mother. Maybe he had a right to be angry that he hadn't seen her in over a month or that she hadn't called more than a handful of times, but at the moment none of that mattered. She was his mother and he missed her.

"Will you tell Gabe that I have an emergency?" Louis said, looking at Roger. "I'll be back in twenty minutes."

"What's wrong?"

"I think my mom's in the stands," Louis said. "I haven't seen her in a while."

Roger and Mickey exchanged a look, and then Roger pointed at the door that led to the concourse.

"Go," he said. "I'll cover for you."

Louis smiled a thankful smile and headed for the door. As he stepped into the concourse, he paused and glanced back. Roger was gone, and Mickey was once again slumped on his bench, one hand clutching his wounded hip, all alone in the empty locker room.

And then the door slammed shut. Louis started down the concourse, and he had taken only a dozen steps when he heard the groan of the crowd, and people began flooding down the walkways from the stands. The bottom of the inning must have just ended. Louis fought his way around the stadium, trying to ignore the curious stares at his uniform, and cut into the stands near the third-base bag. He had guessed correctly; the woman was sitting a few rows below him. She was wearing a plain blue jacket, her long brown hair flowing down her back and a tiny pair of binoculars in her hand.

Louis slowly walked down the concrete steps and cut into her empty row. He was only a few feet away when she turned her face to him. Bryce had been right—it was his mother. She looked surprised to see him.

"Hi, baby," she said, an awkward smile on her face.

"What are you doing here?" Louis asked.

"I promised you that I'd come."

Louis was silent. She patted the seat next to her, and Louis reluctantly settled, his eyes playing over the crowd. The only part of the park that was close to full were the lower stands in right field, which were packed with souvenir hunters hoping to catch Roger's record-breaking home run ball.

"I've been to a couple of games," his mother said after an awkward pause. "I saw one against Cleveland where Maris hit a home run and one against Chicago when he hit two."

"I thought that you didn't like baseball."

"I like watching you in the dugout. You run around like a water bug. And it looks like the players are really nice to you."

Louis turned toward his mother. She was watching him, one hand clutching the armrest of the seat between them.

"I never would have even known you were here if it weren't for Bryce," Louis said, his voice unsteady. "I thought that you wanted to come to a game with *me*."

"I do, baby. But things are . . . complicated."

"You always say that things are complicated," Louis said, his voice rising. "But what's so complicated about using a phone or taking a train to White Plains? I take the train three times a week!"

She moved her hand to his arm. "I want to see you, Louis. I do."

"Then see me. Come to Parents' Day at my school. On Friday."

His mother smiled, a few lines of water running down her face as her eyes wrinkled. "It won't embarrass you to have your friends meet your weird mother?"

"I want you to come," Louis said. "It's important."

"Then I'll be there," she said.

Her hand slipped from the arm of the chair to the back of his jersey. Louis leaned toward her, and as her arm tightened around him and her lips brushed his forehead, he briefly forgave her for disappearing over and over and over.

CHAPTER SIXTEEN

Bottom of the Eighth

Parents' Day at the White Plains Middle School began with an assembly in the gym. As Louis expected, his father had to work, and his stepmother drove Louis and Bryce to school. At the door of the gym she brusquely kissed Louis on the forehead.

"Find me after the assembly if your mother doesn't come," she said. "I'll drop by your classroom after I see Bryce's art project."

"She'll be here," Louis said with much more conviction than he actually felt. He had expected that his mother would call the house to confirm, but he had heard nothing since he had seen her at the stadium.

The assembly began with a song by Bryce and the other eighth graders. Louis sat on the waxy wood floor with his classmates and scanned the packed bleachers, searching for the telltale long hair and dark sweater. But she wasn't there. The assembly lasted twenty minutes, and when it was over the crowd flooded down from the bleachers, and the gym floor overflowed with kids reuniting with their parents. Louis turned and trudged toward the door. It was going to be a long day.

"Hi, baby," a voice said behind him.

Louis turned, and for a long moment he was confused. A woman who looked like his mother was standing in front of him, but this woman had gathered her hair under a large hat and was wearing a lime-green dress and a thin strand of pearls.

"Sorry I'm late," the woman said. "The train took forever."

It sounded like his mother. Louis slowly blinked his eyes, wondering if his imagination was playing a trick on him. He hadn't seen his mother in a dress since their last Christmas in Teaneck, and even then she'd only lasted half a day before changing.

"You look like you've seen a ghost," she said. "I promised you I'd come, didn't I?"

Louis finally found his tongue. "What are you wearing?"

"Camouflage." She twirled, a smile on her face. "I thought it might help."

Louis stared at the pearls, still confused. "I don't care that you don't dress like the other mothers."

"Sure you do," she said. "And it's okay. I know that kids can be mean . . . when I was in sixth grade, I got sick one afternoon, and for the rest of the year everyone called me 'Green Jean.' I hated that name."

Louis smiled. "Some of the kids at my old school called me 'Gooey Louie.' But nobody here knows my name, so they can't make fun of it yet."

His mother grabbed his hand and pulled him toward the door. "Come on," she said. "I want to see your classroom."

The halls were crowded with students and their parents. Louis's classroom was on the second floor, and Louis, like most of the other kids, sat on the carpet while his mother squeezed into his small desk. Mrs. Arrington, his English teacher, entered the room just before the first bell. She was wearing a black skirt and severe brown blouse, and she stood at her usual spot in front of the blackboard and examined the crowded classroom, her nose slightly wrinkled as if something smelly was in the air.

"Welcome," she said in a tone that wasn't very welcoming. "Your children have been working very hard in the seventh grade, and I want to outline what we'll be studying over the remainder of the year."

As Mrs. Arrington launched into one of her long monologues, Louis let his eyes wander around the classroom. Joey was sitting on the floor a few rows in front of him, and when he noticed Louis, he dramatically rolled his eyes. Louis barely managed to suppress a laugh. Joey had gotten him in trouble a couple of times already—he always seemed to get bored at exactly the same moment as Louis, and he was a master at making funny faces.

"There's a question in the back," Mrs. Arrington said.

Louis glanced away from Joey, curious to discover which parent had interrupted Mrs. Arrington's speech, and was horrified to discover that his own mother's arm was the one waving in the air.

"I notice that you're doing a poetry section," his mother said. "Will you be reading any contemporary poets?"

"Several," Mrs. Arrington said. "Robert Frost, obviously. And E. E. Cummings."

"What about the Beats?" his mother asked. "The San Francisco renaissance? The New York school?"

Mrs. Arrington's lips pursed the way they usually did just before she would send a kid to the principal's office. "I don't think those authors are appropriate for children."

"I have to disagree," Louis's mother said. "Shouldn't we be teaching our children about what's actually happening in the world? This is such a fascinating time to be alive. Shouldn't they be exposed to that?"

Kids were beginning to turn around and stare at Louis and his mother, and Louis's instinct was to sink into the floor. But he forced himself to remain motionless and stare at Mrs. Arrington. Louis wasn't sorry that his mother was different. He was sorry that she didn't call or visit him more, but when he had asked her to come to Parents' Day, she had put on a dress and taken the train—even though she hated it in White Plains. So the very least he could do was hold his head up high.

"You're Louis's mother," Mrs. Arrington finally said.

"That's right."

"Louis is a bright young man. I don't think that you should be corrupting him with beatniks and their indecent works."

His mother smiled tightly. "I trust my son. And because I trust him, I think that my job is to expose him to the world and let him decide for himself what is indecent and what is not." She paused. "But we will have to agree to disagree."

It looked as if Mrs. Arrington wanted to say more—a lot more—but she just nodded and returned to her monologue.

Joey gave Louis a horrified glance and then turned to face the board. Louis knew what Joey's expression meant. The first rule of middle school was that you should never, *ever*, stand out. Not unless you were prepared to face the consequences. And Louis's mother had certainly made him stand out.

The rest of Parents' Day was uneventful. Louis's history and math and science teachers gave short presentations, and his mother refrained from asking any more questions. Parents were supposed to leave before lunch, and Louis walked his mother down to the front of the school. She kissed him good-bye, and as they separated, Louis's stepmother emerged from the front door. She raised an eyebrow when she noticed his mother.

"I'm glad you made it," she said. "Louis was nervous when you were late."

"It was nice to see his school," his mother said, her voice missing its usual playful energy.

His stepmother gave the green dress a long look. "I don't think I've ever seen you in something so . . . conservative."

"It's a special occasion." The back of her fingers brushed Louis's cheek. "I've got to get back to the city, baby. I'll see you soon."

"Can I give you a ride to the train station?" Louis's stepmother asked.

His mother shook her head. "I'm happy to walk."

As she turned and started down the school's long driveway, Louis's stepmother put a hand on his shoulder. Louis almost jumped out of his skin. She rarely touched him.

"I'm glad that your mother came," she said.

"So am I."

There was a brief, awkward pause. Her hand was still on his shoulder. "Are you okay?"

"Yes, ma'am."

"Enjoy the rest of your day," she said. "I'll see you at home."

She headed toward the parking lot, and Louis went into the cafeteria for lunch. They were serving macaroni and cheese, which was known among the kids at the school as "mac and yack," and when Louis was done eating, he went outside for recess. Joey was waiting in a quiet corner of the yard with Strat-O-Matic baseball. They played a few innings, and Louis was up 3-1 when Joey glanced behind him and suddenly stiffened. Louis turned. Doug and Alex, who Louis now knew were the two toughest guys in seventh grade, were staring at him.

"Hey," Doug said. "What's the deal with your mother?"

Joey gave Louis a *you're-on-your-own* look and started shoving the game back into its box.

"What do you mean?" Louis asked.

"What was that stuff that made Mrs. Arrington so mad?"

"My mom's a poet." Louis knew that he was digging a deeper hole for himself, but he figured that at this point he was in pretty deep already. "She was talking about some other poets in New York and California."

"Your mom lives in New York?" Doug asked.

Louis nodded. "In the East Village."

"My brother says that only freaks live in the East Village," Alex said.

"I like it down there," Louis said. "It's cool."

Joey grabbed the game and took a few steps backward—as

if he were afraid of being in the splatter zone. Doug glanced at him and then back at Louis.

"Do you visit your mom?" he asked.

"Sometimes."

"What's it like?"

"Different from White Plains. There are all sorts of people . . . black and Chinese and Irish and Italian. And some men wear sandals or have big beards, and lots of women keep their hair long and straight."

"Everyone here dresses the same," Doug said.

"It's easy to go if you want," Louis said. "Just take the train to Grand Central and switch onto the subway."

Doug looked at Louis skeptically. "You take the subway by yourself?"

"Sure. I took it all summer to Yankee Stadium."

"He's a batboy for the Yankees," Joey said. He had been inching back toward the conversation, but he froze as everyone stared at him.

"We know," Alex said.

Joey glanced at Louis, once again nervous, and Louis spoke quickly. "I can probably get you guys into a game or something."

"The season's almost over," Alex said.

Louis shrugged. "Then maybe next spring."

"That would be cool," Alex said.

"Yeah," Doug said.

The two friends turned and walked back toward the school, and when they were a dozen feet away Doug made a comment and they both laughed. But Louis, who was something of an expert on the subject, was pretty sure that they weren't laughing at him. Joey slowly settled back down onto the bench.

"I thought that they were going to pull your underwear up to your ears," he said as he opened the Strat-O-Matic box.

"So did I," Louis said. He smiled. "It's nice to be wrong."

CHAPTER SEVENTEEN

Top of the Ninth

That weekend the Yankees played the Red Sox in their final series of the regular season—three games and three last chances for Roger to hit a home run and break his tie with the Babe. In the first game the Red Sox starting pitcher was Bill Monbouquette, and Bill, who seemed determined to do anything to avoid giving up the record, pitched away from Roger all night. The next afternoon against the Red Sox's promising rookie Don Schwall, Roger got a single, walked once, and grounded out twice.

Everything therefore came down to the final game of the season on Sunday. Would Roger Maris end up tied with Babe Ruth, or would he have his own spot in the record book—with or without an asterisk? Louis barely slept on Saturday night, and when he arrived at the stadium, it seemed as if even the weather gods were excited because it was an absolutely perfect afternoon for baseball. The air was so crisp and clear that Louis thought he could see every blade of the outfield grass, and home plate glowed like a spotlight in the autumn sun.

Despite the perfect weather and Roger's chance to break the record, only twenty-three thousand fans came to the game. Louis thought that maybe the fans were saving themselves for the World Series, which would start at Yankee Stadium the following Wednesday. The stands in right field, however, were once again packed. If Roger broke the record, a restaurant owner from California had offered to pay five thousand dollars for the ball, and a teeming crowd of souvenir hunters swarmed into the park the moment the gates opened to jockey for position.

The clubhouse was subdued before the game. Mickey was in the hospital because doctors had been forced to cut open the wound on his hip to clean out the infection. Nobody was sure whether he would be able to play in the World Series. Roger had also been keeping to himself. He repeatedly told the reporters that he would be honored to finish the season tied with the Babe, but Louis could tell by the strain in his voice and his nervous fidgeting how much he wanted the record.

The Red Sox starting pitcher was Tracy Stallard, a tall rookie from Virginia. In the bottom of the first, with Tony Kubek on base and one out, Roger came up and the crowd rose to its feet. The second pitch was on the outside part of the plate, but Roger started his swing too late and hit a lazy fly to left field. The crowd settled back down, and for the next two and a half innings the park felt sleepy. Both pitchers were mowing through the opposing lineups, and even the players seemed more interested in soaking up the warm sun than focusing on the game.

But that changed when Roger strode to the plate with one out in the fourth inning. The right-field stands once again looked like Grand Central Station at rush hour, and Louis stood on the top step of the dugout with most of the players to get a better view. The first pitch, a curveball, was high and outside. Roger let it go. The second pitch, a fastball, was low and inside. Roger let that one go too. A few scattered boos came from the stands.

"They're not giving him anything," Clete Boyer muttered next to Louis. "It's been junk for three days."

Louis kept his eyes focused on Stallard. The Red Sox pitcher fiddled with the resin bag and then climbed back onto the rubber and peered at the catcher for the sign. Something about the set of his jaw told Louis that Clete was wrong—Stallard wanted to throw a strike. He didn't want to nibble around the plate or surrender a walk. He wanted to get Roger out.

Stallard started his windup, and Louis leaned forward, his own jaw clenched. It was a fastball, waist-high, and Roger swung hard, his neck and shoulders straining with the effort. As the ball left the bat a ferocious roar burst from the crowd, and Louis tracked the ball against the bright blue sky, his eyes squinting against the sun. He had seen Roger hit dozens of home runs in batting practice and games, but his brain nevertheless kept double-checking the math. Was it high enough? Was it far enough? Was the wind blowing too hard? Was luck on Roger's side?

And then the ball landed ten rows deep in the chaos of the right-field stands, and Louis leaped out of the dugout, his arm punching the air. He instinctively started toward home plate, but then he remembered the rules and froze, uncertain. A hand tugged on his uniform. It was Gabe.

"Sorry," Louis shouted over the thunder from the crowd. "I'll get back in the dugout."

Gabe was smiling. "Go get his bat. And shake his hand."

Louis turned and sprinted out to the bat. He picked it up and then waited next to Yogi Berra at home plate as Roger slowly trotted around the bases. Photographers and security men were crowded around the infield, but a young kid somehow managed to break through the cordon and dashed up to Roger as he came down the third-base line. Roger paused to shake his hand before continuing the last ten feet and deliberately stepping on home plate. He slapped Yogi's hand and then looked at Louis.

"You did it!" Louis yelled, his voice barely audible over the cascading roar from the stands. "You did it!"

"I guess I did," Roger said.

He was smiling in a way that Louis thought he recognized. It was as if a weight had been lifted from his shoulders, and he wasn't sure yet if he should be happy or sad or relaxed or scared. But Roger couldn't do what Louis liked to do and creep off to a quiet corner to figure it out—he was standing in front of twenty-three thousand screaming fans.

Roger gave Louis a last glance and then walked back toward the dugout. The players were still on the top step, and as Roger tried to slip inside they barred his way. He tried again, but they shoved him back out onto the field.

"Take a bow," Kubek shouted. "You think that someone breaks the Babe's record every day?"

Roger stared at Kubek for a second before taking a few quick steps away from the dugout. He lifted the cap from his head and tipped it to the crowd, and then slowly bowed four times. The cheers rose like swelling waves with each bow, and when the fourth one came the roar echoed from every empty corner of the stadium. Roger smiled again, this time with none of the reserve that Louis had seen before, and then he slipped into the dugout and took his usual seat on the bench.

The ball had sparked a furious brawl when it landed in the stands, and Sal Durante, a nineteen-year-old truck driver from Brooklyn, had been the one who emerged with the prize. He offered the ball to Roger for free—which would mean passing on the five thousand dollars from the restaurant owner—but Roger refused. "The boy's planning to get married and he can use the money," Roger said when the reporters asked him why he had turned down the gift. "It shows there are still some good people left in the world after all."

In the clubhouse after the game Roger took pictures with Sal and the ball and a special Yankees jersey with the number 61 on the back. When the photographers were finished, he sat in front of his locker for at least an hour and patiently answered questions from a pack of fifty or sixty reporters. Louis was busy with other tasks, but he overheard one long answer.

"Whether I beat Ruth's record or not is for others to say. Babe Ruth was a big man in baseball, maybe the biggest ever. I'm not saying I am of his caliber, but I'm glad to say I hit more than he did in a season. And maybe the sixty-first wasn't in a hundred and fifty-four games, but I'm happy. That's the way it was to be and that's the way it is."

The crowd of reporters gradually began to dwindle, and

one of the other players brought Roger a beer. Louis was almost finished with his chores when Gabe pulled him aside.

"Skip wants to see you," he said.

Louis's forehead wrinkled. He'd spoken to Mr. Houk maybe ten times all season, and he'd never been called into the manager's office. Had he done something wrong? Was it because he'd run onto the field after Roger's home run? Louis slowly walked down the hall, his mind racing, and found Mr. Houk sitting at his desk with paperwork scattered in front of him. The tattered remains of a cigar were sticking out of the corner of his mouth.

"Come in," he said to Louis. "And shut the door."

Louis followed the instructions and then stood uncertainly in front of the desk, his hands clasped behind his back. Mr. Houk pushed the papers to the side and gave Louis a long look.

"You've done a great job for us this season," he said. "Gabe tells me that you've worked as hard as any batboy we've ever had. And the fellows really like having you around. Especially Rog and Mick."

Louis could feel his cheeks tightening as he smiled. "Thank you, sir."

"But I'm afraid I have some bad news." As Louis's smile disappeared, Mr. Houk shuffled though the stack of papers and pulled out a single sheet. "I got a letter from the commissioner this morning. He wants all of the batboys for the World Series to be at least fifteen years old. He thinks it will look more professional on television."

"You mean I can't be a batboy in the World Series?" Louis asked. It felt as if someone had punched him in the stomach.

Mr. Houk tossed the letter aside. "Frankly, I think it's ridiculous. I was going to lie about your age, but one of the reporters ratted you out to the commissioner's office. Nathan Scully from the *Daily News*."

Louis swallowed hard. "I understand."

"I wasn't blowing smoke, son. You did a great job for us this year. You call us in the spring if you want to do it again, and we'll find a spot for you."

Louis managed to nod, and then he turned, opened the office door, and stepped into the hall. The locker room was almost empty, and Louis slowly changed from his uniform into his plain brown pants and white collared shirt. As he tossed the uniform into the laundry pile he felt something catch in the back of his throat. It had felt good to wear the Yankees pinstripes—like he was part of something bigger than just himself. Like he was part of a family.

"Hey," a voice said from across the locker room. "You're still here."

It was Roger. He had emerged from the showers wearing only a towel and his white sandals with his name stenciled across the top. He padded over to his locker, and Louis waited until he was wearing a pair of pants to cross the room.

"Congratulations, Mr. Maris," Louis said, his hand extended.

Roger's huge hand encircled Louis's. "Thanks, kid. But you don't have to be so formal."

"Yes, sir."

Roger pulled on his shirt, his fingers fumbling with the buttons. "Gabe told me about the World Series. You know, I don't know if I hate that commissioner more for his stupid asterisk or kicking you out. And don't worry about Nathan Scully. Me and the boys will figure out some way to get back at him."

"It's okay," Louis said. "I don't mind so much."

Roger gave him a quizzical look. "Really?"

"Sure," Louis said. "It will be fun to be just a fan during the World Series. And I already saw the best part of this season. I already saw you hit sixty-one home runs."

"You better be back next spring," Roger said. "I can't imagine trying to face the wolves without my lucky batboy."

"I will," Louis said. "And tell Mr. Mantle that I hope he feels better."

Roger smiled. "Ah, he'll be okay. He's finally got New York on his side."

The smile slowly faded, and Roger stared off into the far reaches of the locker room. He had the same lost expression that Louis had seen on the field after the home run.

"Are you okay, Mr. Maris?" Louis asked.

Roger shook his head as if he was trying to clear out cobwebs.

"I'm just tired," he said. "Some people are born for the big stage. Mickey and Whitey . . . they love the reporters and the crowds and the attention. Me, I just love baseball. I love hitting and fielding and hanging out in the dugout with the guys. All that other stuff is just something you have to deal with if you want to play pro ball."

Roger shook his head again, his eyes still unfocused, and Louis suddenly realized that he was really talking to himself.

"I'll never know why some people didn't want me to hit sixty-one home runs," he said. "I'll never know why even some Yankee fans booed me. But I do know this. When I came back to the dugout and was sitting alone on that bench, I was proud. Proud that my kids will spend the rest of their lives knowing that their daddy did something that nobody else has ever done. It's kind of like what I said to Mickey that time in the locker room. I play for my family, and I play because I love the game."

"I love the game too," Louis said. "I wish I was better at it."

"You don't have to be great at baseball to love it." Roger paused. "I can make you one promise, Louis. Maybe you won't be a professional ballplayer, but if you try as hard at life as you tried in this clubhouse—if you're this funny and smart and resourceful—you'll be a success. You understand?"

"Yeah," Louis said.

Roger reached into his locker, pulled out a bat, and held it out to Louis.

"Here," he said. "A little present. Me and the boys signed it."

Louis stared at the bat for a long moment, and his hands were shaking when he finally reached out and took it. His eyes traced the first few signatures: Tony Kubek, Mickey Mantle, Elston Howard, Whitey Ford . . .

"Should I take it back?" Roger asked, his voice teasing. "Or can I tell the boys that you liked it?"

"I love it," Louis said.

"Good." Roger slipped a coat over his shoulders. "I've got to go have dinner with my wife. And visit Mickey in the hospital."

"Bye," Louis said.

"Keep your chin up," Roger said. "And remember . . . it

doesn't matter that you won't be in the clubhouse during the World Series. As far as Mickey and I are concerned, you'll always be an M&M Boy."

A moment later he disappeared out the door, and Louis was alone in the locker room. He glanced down at the bat. Just a few months ago those names had been merely statistics on a baseball card, but now each signature reminded him of a story. Pranks and fights and clutch hits and great plays. Louis hoped that in the years to come he would remember everything, but if he could keep just one memory it would be of the expression on Roger's face that afternoon. His wonder and fear after doing something that nobody else had ever done—something that nobody had ever expected him to do.

And in that moment, alone in that locker room, Louis hoped that sometime in his life he would have the same feeling. Maybe it would be baseball or maybe it would be something else. Maybe he would be fifteen or maybe fifty. And if it ever happened—no matter when or how—Louis knew that he would always owe a debt to a quiet, serious ballplayer named Roger Maris.

CHAPTER EIGHTEEN

Bottom of the Ninth

The World Series between the Yankees and the Reds began as a nail-biter and ended as a rout. The teams split the first two games in Yankee Stadium, but the Yankees swept the three games in Cincinnati, winning the final one 13-5 to seize their nineteenth championship. Roger, aside from the winning home run in game three, was quiet in the series, and Mickey was so sick that he played in only two games. But Whitey Ford pitched brilliantly in his starts, and the other players helped carry the load as the 1961 Yankees earned their place among the greatest teams of all time.

Louis watched all five games with Bryce and his father. They went to Yankee Stadium for the first game—a 2-0 win—and saw the rest on television. It was strange to be so removed from the team, to see them from the stands or through the filter of a flickering black-and-white image. But it still felt good when they won, especially after the disaster against the Pirates the previous fall, and when the final out fell into Hector Lopez's glove, Louis celebrated without regrets or reservations.

Louis's birthday was the Saturday after the Yankees won the Series, and he asked his father if his mother could come to lunch. After taking a few days to consider the question his father said yes, and his mother made plans to arrive in White Plains on the noon train. Louis went down to meet her at the station. She was one of the last people to step onto the platform, and when she finally emerged, Louis sprinted toward her and leaped into her waiting hug. Her usual outfit had replaced the green dress from Parents' Day, but Louis didn't care. He was just glad that she had made it.

Lunch was the nice kind of boring. His mother asked his stepmother for the recipe for the chicken, even though she hated to cook, and his stepmother asked his mother about a show at the Museum of Fine Arts, even though she never went to museums, and pretty soon they were singing "Happy Birthday" and nobody had gotten in a fight.

"Did you make a wish?" his father asked after Louis blew out the candles on his cake.

"Yeah," Louis said. He paused. "I wished that we could all be together for Thanksgiving. And maybe Christmas."

Louis could tell from the glances among the adults at the table that he had pushed his luck. His stepmother spoke first. She was looking at his mother.

"We'd love to have you here," she said. "And I know

it would mean a lot to Louis. It was hard for him last Christmas."

"I know it was," his mother said. Her hand covered Louis's on the table. "I'll try, baby. Okay?"

"Okay," Louis said.

They were quiet for a minute, and then his father suggested that Louis open his presents. His father and stepmother had gotten him a new mitt, and his mother had found a copy of the *1960 Little Red Book of Baseball*, which had the official records—except for the one Roger had just broken, of course. But his mother had carefully typed out a special page and glued it to the back cover that read: "Roger Maris, *New York Yankees*. Single Season Record of 61 Home Runs. 1961."

When he was done opening the presents, Louis walked his mother back to the train station. They sat quietly on a bench, until the loudspeaker crackled and the agent announced that the train was approaching.

"I'll try to come at Thanksgiving," she said as they stood. "I promise."

"You should come more," Louis said.

She smiled sadly. "I want to come more. But it's important for you to be happy out here. You have a new family now. And a new mother."

"She's not my mother," Louis said. The train had pulled into the station, and Louis waited for the squeals from the tracks to fall silent before continuing. "Now that baseball season is over, I want to visit you in New York. A lot."

"I'd like that, baby. But we'll have to ask your father."

"I'm old enough," Louis said. "If I could take the train to

the stadium, I can take the train to your apartment."

"We'll figure it out." She pulled him into a hug, squeezing him so tightly that it was hard to breathe. As they separated, she held him at arm's length and looked him up and down. "You're getting so big. In another year you'll be as tall as I am."

"I love you," Louis said.

"I love you, too," she said.

The doors of the train slid open, and a moment later she was inside. Louis caught a last glimpse of her face through the smudged glass, and then the train pulled out of the station and she was gone. Louis waited until the train had rounded the far bend and disappeared before slowly walking home. Bryce was on the porch when Louis got back to the house, a bat in one hand and a glove in the other.

"We're playing stickball," he said. "You want to come?"

"Sure," Louis said.

Bryce looked shocked and Louis almost laughed—Bryce had probably asked the question figuring that there was no way that Louis would say yes.

"Don't worry," Louis said with a smile. "I'll play on the other team."

It was a chilly fall day, and Louis put on a thick sweatshirt and a pair of canvas pants before grabbing his new glove. By the time he got to the vacant lot, the teams were almost full.

"He's with you," Bryce said to Kenny, who was the other team's captain.

Kenny looked at Louis as if he were covered in slugs. "We don't want him."

"Are you kidding?" Bryce asked. "He's been getting

lessons from Roger Maris and Mickey Mantle! I was just trying to make sure the teams were even."

For a long moment the baseball diamond was silent. Kenny's mouth flopped open and closed like a fish.

"Maris and Mantle?" he finally asked, his voice halting.

"Louis is a batboy for the Yankees. Didn't you know?"

Something about Bryce's tone suggested that Kenny must be a very bad Yankees fan if he didn't know that Louis was a batboy, and Kenny looked simultaneously embarrassed, surprised, and overwhelmed.

"I'll play right," Louis said.

Kenny quickly nodded. "Okay."

For two innings Louis didn't touch a ball or bat, but in the top of the third Bryce hit a grounder past first base. Louis charged in, picked it up, and threw it to second in time to hold him to a single—which earned him a few compliments from his teammates and a friendly glare from Bryce. Louis was nevertheless glad that nobody had hit him anything in the air because it was hard to see the ball against the slate-gray sky.

In the bottom of the third Louis finally came up to bat. His team was down a run, and there was one out and nobody on base. Louis carefully scuffed a hole for his front foot, the way he'd seen Roger do a thousand times, and then settled into a crouch, the bat hovering above his shoulders. He could feel the weight of his teammates' stares. They all expected him to strike out. The usual stream of obnoxious comments was coming from the opposing fielders, and Bryce was standing on the pitching mound, a cocky smile on his face.

Remember what Roger and Bob and Mickey said, Louis

told himself. *It's just you and the ball. And don't close your eyes.*

Bryce started his windup, and the ball began its circular journey from his glove to his ear and then toward the plate. Louis's hands whipped forward, his hips moving in perfect unison with the bat, and his brain focused only on the white blur of stitches and leather. . . .

THE END

WES TOOKE lives in California with his wife and dog. He has written a novel about baseball for adults, along with articles for various publications. This is his first book for middle graders. You can visit him at westooke.com.